WE ALL LOVED
COWBOYS

WE ALL LOVED COWBOYS

Carol Bensimon

Translated from the Portuguese by
Beth Fowler

TRANSIT BOOKS

Published by Transit Books
2301 Telegraph Avenue, Oakland, California 94612
www.transitbooks.org

© Carol Bensimon 2013
Translation copyright © Beth Fowler 2018
First published in Portuguese as *Todo nos adoravamos caubois* by Companhia das
Letras in 2013

The rights of Carol Bensimon and Beth Fowler to be identified respectively as
author and translator of this work have been identified in accordance with Section
77 of the Copyright, Designs and Patents Act 1988.

LIBRARY OF CONGRESS CONTROL NUMBER: 2018955089

DESIGN & TYPESETTING
Justin Carder

DISTRIBUTED BY
Consortium Book Sales & Distribution
(800) 283-3572 | cbsd.com

Printed in the United States of America

9 8 7 6 5 4 3 2 1

Work published with the support of the Brazilian Ministry of Culture / National
Library Foundation
Obra publicada com o apoio do Ministério da Cultura do Brasil / Fundação
Biblioteca Nacional

MINISTÉRIO DA CULTURA
Fundação BIBLIOTECA NACIONAL

WE ALL LOVED
COWBOYS

1.

ALL WE DID WAS TAKE THE BR-116, passing beneath bridges that showed slogans of cities we hadn't the slightest intention of visiting, or which told of Christ's return or counted down to the end of the world. We left behind the suburban streets whose beginnings are marked by the highway and which then disappear in an industrial estate or among the abandoned shacks along a stream where stray dogs crawl and rarely bark, and we carried on, on until the straight road turned a corner. I was driving. Julia had her feet on the dashboard. I could only look at her occasionally. When she didn't know the words to the song, she hummed instead. "You've changed your hair," I said, glancing at her bangs. Julia replied: "About two years ago, Cora." We laughed as we climbed into the hills. That was the start of our journey.

My car had been out of action for some time, under a silver waterproof cover, like a big secret you just can't hide or a child trying to disappear by putting her hands over her eyes, surrounded by junk in the garage at my mother's house. Initially, mom was desperate to resolve the situation. It's a bad business leaving a car off the road for so long, she would say, although she understood very little about business and even less about getting rid of things. She lived in a house that already seemed too big when there were still three of us. When you opened certain closets in that house, you could see the entire evolution of ladies-wear from the mid-sixties onwards. Lovely jackets, pretty dresses that didn't fit mom anymore. I was direct about the car. I said: "Maybe I'll come back." I could sense her breath crossing the ocean and almost capsizing before returning to dry land. Perhaps it was a mistake to offer hope to a single mother, given that I wasn't even considering the possibility of moving home at that point. We never spoke about the car again.

Three years later, I was back and found the garage fuller than ever, so much so that I could barely see the terracotta floor tiles for the bags full of papers, the boxes of all sizes. There were dust rollers, an electric heater, a small bicycle, a minibar missing a leg. I got the impression I could have written "wash me" in the air with my index finger. I pushed open the wooden concertina doors and let in the light. I stood looking at the street for a while. It was no longer the same street, I mean, it was the same street, but in place of the houses belonging to my childhood friends—where were they now?—an apartment block had been built. It scared me to think that one person's aesthetic preferences could be summed up in that white, seventeen story mastodon, which stood out on the block like a naked woman in an order of nuns, or a nun at the First Brazilian Meeting of Polyamorists.

Apart from that, there were other subtle changes to that section of the street. They, however, did not date from the last three years, the three years I had spent away from Porto Alegre and that house, during which time I had rarely imagined my return and the exhausting list of comparisons that would almost certainly stem from it. For some reason, what I was trying to do was rebuild the street of my adolescence and my difficulty in achieving that made me think about those little books you get in Rome where, by superimposing two images, you can see something that was once grandiose where now there are only remains of columns, marble blocks or a sizeable area of grass.

Then I went back into the garage. I pulled the waterproof cover off the car. It was very clean. A strange, metallic blue body in the midst of all that dusty chaos. The battery, though, or whatever it was, had gone to pot.

Even though the car was unfit to drive off right then, I adjusted the back of the seat and stayed sitting there. I very nearly put my hands on the wheel. But cars weren't my obsession. I would never enter the word "cars" on a form asking about my interests. You ask me what model just went past and I'll never be able to tell you. It was their mobility that appealed to me, mobility as an end. And I thought about how obscure that is when you are first presented with a car, how, at eighteen, with your driver's license in a flawless plastic sheath and that ridiculous photo with the haircut you'll regret later, all you want to do is cruise along open roads at dawn without ever getting anywhere. Or rather, your anywhere is an album to be heard in full, your anywhere is a river you watch as you smoke, with as many friends as you can fit in the back seat. The strange thing is that keeping these habits beyond their expiry date makes them seem, in the eyes of others, to be nothing more than a sign of eccentricity in someone who never knew how to grow up, who never let a car achieve its full functionality, its raison d'être: taking you from A to B in the quickest, most comfortable way possible.

That was the kind of thing that could annoy me. My mother entered the garage as I was reminiscing. In the rearview mirror, I saw her running her fingers over the dust-covered boxes, head bowed, giving the impression that she was reading what might be written there, as if until that moment she had ignored their contents or didn't even know why they were piled up in her garage. I got out of the car and waited for her to approach. She gave me one of her out-of-context smiles. "Won't it start?" It was quite common for bad news to come out of my mother's mouth accompanied by a smile. Not out of spite, quite the opposite; there was some notion of compensation in it.

"I think it would have been a miracle if it had," I said.

We agreed that it probably wasn't anything serious, nothing a mechanic couldn't sort with the turn of a spanner. We stayed standing there. I looked around me. Funny I couldn't remember that tiny bicycle. No one other than me had been a child in this house.

"Is Julia going with you?"

"Mmhm."

"I thought you'd fallen out."

It was a bicycle with stabilizers and there was a bell attached to the handlebar.

"I thought you weren't speaking anymore. You had a fight once, didn't you?"

"Yes. But it's all fine now."

I asked what was in all those boxes. Mom raised her eyebrows and looked down. They were papers she had collected from the office. She opened a box, as if she needed to illustrate what she was saying. I saw part of a beige folder labeled "Invoices 2002." The box was probably full of them, right to the bottom. Only the years changed.

"Do you miss the office?"

She thought about it.

"I miss having an obligation to leave the house."

I rang Julia four days later from a gas station. The sky was blue, it was Saturday, the clouds glided until they scattered into pieces. I asked her to wait for me in front of the hotel. The attendant soon finished filling my tank and I left.

All great ideas seem like bad ones at some point.

Julia was staying in one of those little hotels in the center. Not the kind that has decayed to the point of being considered elegant, but something a bit more functional, near the bus station, frequented by executives in suits too broad for their shoulders. There were half a dozen of those right at the entrance, laughing loudly as they milled about the red carpet, rather worn in the middle but in good condition at the edges. A cluster of fake palm trees, too, whose plastic leaves looked more rigid than Tupperware, gave a tropical welcome to those arriving by car at the main door. Julia was waiting for me next to one of the palms. She was wearing a denim jacket buttoned up to the neck and burgundy skinny jeans. She had radically changed her hair; it fell to her shoulders in a slight wave and thick bangs hung over her forehead, almost covering her eyebrows. Never in a million years would you guess that this girl had grown up in the depths of Rio Grande do Sul.

She was biting her cuticles. That hadn't changed. When Julia saw me, the tip of her finger was released from between her teeth, she nodded, grabbed her bag by the handle and walked towards me. I got out of the car. She was from Soledade, Capital of Precious Stones—all cities in the interior feel the need to proclaim themselves capital of something and naturally the reason for their singularity is a compulsory source of pride for their residents. So there was no one in Soledade who didn't see in an amethyst coaster or a rose-quartz obelisk the most beautiful, sensitive art.

I received a lengthy embrace and a "Paris was good to you," a subject I thought best to hold at bay with a stock smile. A few yards away, a man wearing the baggy gaucho trousers known as *bombachas* was watching us with a certain sad interest.

For a few moments, I imagined what it would have been like if she had been there too, in the small apartment on the Rue du Fauboug du Temple, from which you heard a babble of Chinese voices going about what may well have been their regular business, but which assumed a tense quality due to the fact that I couldn't make out any variety in their intonation. Julia would certainly have liked the grand boulevards, the gilt detailing on the facade of the opera house and a pastry in six perfect shiny layers sitting in the window of a patisserie just as much as she would a metro station in urgent need of renovation or an argumentative beggar raising his finger to an old lady. She was an adaptable girl, who took the best from whatever she was presented with. Take her to any city in the world and, within three months, she'd be calling it home.

We took Julia's bag to the back of the car and positioned it in the trunk, at which point there was time to exchange a few banal questions and answers about how our lives were going. Paris is beautiful, Montreal is freezing, the course is great.

Then we got into the car. The previous day, I had bought a road map of Rio Grande do Sul. I hadn't taken a GPS because receiving any kind of instruction would go against the idea of the trip. I wanted a map on which we could circle the names of towns with a red pen, one that starts tearing at the folds on long journeys. Julia looked at it with a faint smile and shut the door.

"Where are we off to first?"

I replied that we were going to Antônio Prado, up in the hills. Julia began to unfold the map.

"But you've never been there, right?"

"Neither of us has been there."

My attempt to say something of consequence ended with the click of my seatbelt, which only made it sound more ridiculous. To prevent any echo, I added, almost without breathing: "And your parents?"

She laughed.

"Oh, they're pretty furious. Hurt, actually." Julia looked at the map, like someone flicking uninterestedly through a magazine in a white waiting room. "But I don't care about that as much as I used to, you know? They went to live by the beach."

"I know."

"It's nice there, but there's nothing to—"

We were interrupted by three successive knocks on my window. I looked round and recognized the guy in *bombachas*. He was the only person left after all the initial hubbub, other than two employees in kepis, the kind chauffeurs wear, but which definitely seemed to suggest something else, more like a couple of boys dressed up for a carnival dance at the Friends of Tramandaí Society. I lowered the window.

"Those boots you're wearing are for men," he said, pointing into the car, his finger withdrawing and returning twice. From his expression, my boots seemed to have ruined his day.

Slightly shocked, I looked at my feet to check what I was actually wearing, and saw it was my calf-high Doc Martens, for which I had paid a small fortune in one of the brand's stores in Paris. It was too much to expect their counter-cultural connotation would penetrate someone who, at best, had seen boots like this protecting the feet of the military police as they shot rubber bullets into the tents of the Landless Workers' Movement. That's the problem with fashion: you depend on others. If they don't get the message, all your efforts go down the drain.

I let out a short, resigned laugh.

"I hardly think you're a fashion expert."

So there I was, confronting his prematurely wrinkled face, when I felt Julia place a hand on my leg and heard her say quietly that we should get out of there. A few minutes later we were leaving the city on the BR-116, a noisy grey line following the railroads, cutting the suburbs down the middle, which, like any exit route from any big Brazilian city, makes apparent the country's determination to emulate the United States, although what becomes even more apparent is the failure of that mission.

I was still in shock over the incident with the man in *bombachas*, even though I had the strongest convictions about fashion and style, about gender and the rulebook of life. But reading *The Second Sex* or whatever doesn't make you immune to idiotic opinions. To be honest, the thing I found most discomfiting was not knowing exactly what Julia thought about it all. True, she had unleashed her anger once we moved off in the car ("I can't believe he knocked on the window just to give his opinion on your boots!"). True, she had made it clear I shouldn't pay any attention to the words of a stranger ("what an accent he had, my God!") and, on top of that, she thought very differently ("I love your boots"). But that over-effusiveness ended up producing the opposite effect: it increased my distrust.

Meanwhile, outside, the buildings by the edge of the road seemed as though they were being consumed by soot, broken down by a kind of urban erosion, in which two seconds were equivalent to hundreds of years. Some of them held advertising boards showing amateur models in rather grotesque positions, desperately striving to look attractive. If someone appears at one of those windows, I thought, I won't be able to help feeling a twinge of commiseration.

"You'll never guess what was going on in that hotel," said Julia, and I was prepared to continue on that subject, whatever it was, until we recovered our Reserves of Intimacy, frozen some years earlier.

"No idea."

"A meeting of chinchilla breeders."

She started laughing like one of those people who chuckle alone as they walk, and you're never quite sure whether it's because they have earphones in (what could they be listening to that's so funny?).

"They were negotiating pelts with a *Serbian*. Actually, it was two Serbians, father and son. And the teenager was the expert." Julia picked up my iPod. "How do you plug this in?"

"With that cord there," I pointed. "But carry on, please."

"It only gets better."

"I can imagine."

The un-nuanced joy of an indie band dribbled through the speakers like a viscous liquid. I thought: glad we kept the good tunes for when we're leaving the city. Then she continued her story about the chinchillas, which was particularly long and juicy. She had followed almost the entire transaction from a distance, leaning against the entrance to the convention room as the breeders took turns in front of the Serbians. They were carrying suitcases, which they opened on a large table, and they were overflowing with pelts, kind of like chinchillas in plan, chinchillas in 2D, get it? said Julia, to which I replied, yes, unfortunately I could picture it. "So the boy picked up the pelts one by one and smacked them. Sometimes he blew. I think that was how he worked out whether it was a good or a bad pelt. Then each one was given a label with a value. They were separated into piles. So many dollars for this pile, so many dollars for the other, and in the midst of it all there was a redhead interpreter, trying to make them understood, but occasionally someone would get carried away and bang on the table, and she seemed completely lost."

I had been up into the hills many times, when I was a child and my parents still had a bit of energy. In those days, money came in without them having to make much of an effort and turned into articulated Ninja Turtle figures and five star hotels. I never asked for a sibling. My father was an ENT doctor, an *otorrinolaringologista*, twenty-two letters long, five fewer than *inconstitucionalissimamente*, although he insisted his profession was the longest word in the Portuguese language.

"Cora, listen. *Inconstitucionalissimamente* is an adverb."

"So?"

"So, it's not even in the dictionary."

"But it exists."

"It exists, yes, but it's a word whose only use is to be long, understand?"

I really liked having that conversation over and over again.

It was funny the way that my father's professional success gave me the false impression that otorhinolaryngology was booming during that period of my childhood, like pet shops and private security firms today. Not that the whole city was suffering from tonsillitis, sinusitis, and tumors of the ear canal, but everyone who woke up one day coughing or half deaf seemed to have my father's number on their refrigerator door. Because of this, whenever someone mentions the difficult days of frozen savings, the dollar through the roof, all I can think about is how we had it easy in my house at the start of the nineties. This contributed to a curious feeling that I always lived my life upside down; the decline of the majority was my most prosperous period and, when things started to improve around me, I was already in free fall.

When I say the three of us went to the hills frequently, I'm of course talking about the resorts of Canela and Gramado. Few families attempt anything more ambitious than that. On those trips, my father was the guy who drove with his arm hanging outside the car, and my mother was the woman who thought that that posture wasn't correct or safe. My father was the guy who saw a stall and wanted to drink sugar-cane juice and eat cake, and my mother was the woman who reminded him that my aunt and uncle were expecting us for lunch.

Julia and I stopped to eat at a place by the roadside. It was begging to be visited, a pastiche of German architecture, the front of which was overcrowded with flowerpots and garden gnomes and rugs made of squares of hide. We got out of the car and inhaled the fresh mountain air, as if we had spent the last six months in an airless cave. Two easels fixed in the gravel ("Give us a try!") left no doubt that they also served lunch and snacks as well as cheese, salami, honey, phone cards and batteries to take away. "Nice," said Julia. I personally thought that places that sell a bit of everything only highlight the fact that they are unable to prosper in any specific area, but even so, I had to agree. The surroundings, at least, were very pretty. I took a few steps forward and looked at the valley below us, speckled with wooden houses. Chimneys were smoking, dogs were barking, children were running around a girl whose outstretched arms, open palms and short steps gave the impression that she was wearing a blindfold. Julia came up to me, dragging her feet over the gravel.

"Perhaps we should look for something outside town. When we get to Antônio Prado," I said.

"Like cabins?"

I nodded.

"I second that."

Between the ages of eighteen and twenty-one, I think we must have planned the famous Unplanned Journey a hundred times. And when something like that is repeated so often, with minimal variations, it's only natural that everything compacts into a single powerful memory, the setting for which is determined at random—it only needs to have happened once in the place in question—while its dramatic charge comes from the sum of all the nights that eventually led us to the idea of the trip, plus the number of years separating us from those nights. In my case, the memory is this: Julia and me lying on the rug in her spartan room on the third floor of the exclusive Maria Imaculada all-girls residence, where she lived the whole time she was at university. We're looking at the ceiling. To my left, there's a record player that Julia's family was thinking of throwing away, and the vinyl that's spinning once belonged to her brother and brought great delight to the small parties where her parents served Coca-Cola and a boy who was more devious than the rest adulterated his friends' plastic cups with palm fruit *cachaça*. *Houses of the Holy*, Led Zeppelin's 1973 album, lived right between Pink Floyd and Metallica in a typical teenager's bedroom in Soledade, often smelling of the sweat of forgotten soccer shirts under the furniture. But then Julia's brother supposedly stopped listening to music after he got married.

The day we listened to *Houses of the Holy* lying on the floor, we got carried away again over the Unplanned Journey. There was an infinite number of uninteresting towns to be discovered, and that album seemed like fuel for our plans for freedom. But yet again, we didn't leave the room, we didn't run downstairs, we didn't reach the car before the spark went out. To tell the truth, we stayed staring at the ceiling, even though the volume and tone of our voices betrayed a great deal of excitement.

It was as if you'd spent months thinking about whether to dye your hair blue, and suddenly you realize that all that time spent deliberating, analyzing, imagining, has ended up completely satisfying your desire to rebel. And so the trip was left for another time, a safe distance away from disappointment, after all, having blue hair was perhaps not such a great way to break from the status quo and uninteresting places were perhaps just uninteresting places, nothing more. I breathed deeply. It was mountain air, and we were there, five or six years late, but there, finally. We had survived a fight that was still hanging over us, Paris, Montreal, the madness of our families. This journey was another irresistible failure.

2.

I KNEW VERY LITTLE ABOUT ANTÔNIO PRADO. Only that a period movie had been shot there once and they had filled the streets with mud, then left it all behind after they finished filming. When Julia and I arrived at the town, it was already after four. The front windshield was coated with a fine dust. I drove slowly along the cobbles of the main street. We had stopped on the way there to visit, by mutual agreement and in the following order, an old water mill just outside Picada Café, a recreation of a nineteenth-century German colony where Julia had sat on the bench outside the school making vague comments about the lives of immigrants (apparently all the old dead folks' clothes and the narrow beds and the crumpled promissory notes fading in display cases had had the desired effect), then into a green labyrinth that twice brought us to a dead end, and, finally, the old workers' district of Galópolis, where the steeply sloping roofs over brick buildings seemed to anticipate a snow that never fell.

Now, Antônio Prado, a city colonized by Italians, not far from Caxias do Sul. But I wasn't paying attention to details as I drove. I was thinking about a place with cabins. Any place, so long as it had cabins. Julia opened the window.

"Hi, excuse me, I wonder if you could help us."

A dirt track led us to the guesthouse. It was a villa from 1946, the date engraved on the stone foundation in bas-relief, which gave me the strange feeling that people back then must have been thinking about us, or else wouldn't that inscription have seemed rather ridiculous in 1947, looking back like an idiot after just one year? Julia entered first, with me right behind. The old part of the building had been converted into a reception and games room. For a few moments we were alone, not knowing whether to clap our hands, as was traditional in these parts, or do something else to attract attention. To tell the truth, the room was rather suffocating; the hoard of rustic objects, farming tools attached to the ceiling, old lanterns, plates, portraits in oval frames, a Singer sewing machine, made the blue ping-pong table look somewhat out of place.

Suddenly, a woman came out from behind a door. Yes, there were cabins. Yes, some of them were vacant.

Julia began to fill out the register in her careful hand. Every now and then, she raised her head and smiled at the lady. The old woman, in turn, was following my movements around the room with her eyes, as if the collection of objects wasn't meant to be seen close up, more as a brief panorama. Perhaps she was friendlier with other guests. Perhaps she offered strawberry bonbons to kids. But we didn't seem to be the kind of person she took pleasure in serving. What kind of people were we? For starters, I was platinum blonde, tangled hair, an inch or so of intentional brown roots. In addition to the Doc Martens, I was wearing very tight jeans (good legs since I was young), a tank top and a close-fitting red leather jacket with a hood, which, as you'd expect, stood proud behind my neck. And since I'd been living in Paris, I'd been going heavy on the eyeliner.

As for Julia, she naturally had a better chance of raising a friendly response. For one thing, she didn't look as strange as I did. I wouldn't be the least bit surprised if someone suddenly complimented her earrings. Secondly, she was always eager to please, even when she perceived a touch of hostility in the other person. This had often irritated me in the past. And yet Julia also seemed to exude a certain degree of inadequacy, as if only a series of coincidences, a long chain of them, could explain her presence in that place.

Julia asked the lady her name. "Adiles," she replied laconically. I continued my close perusal of that hodgepodge of objects. On one of the walls, there was a sequence of behind-the-scenes photographs from that movie. Patrícia Pilar. Glória Pires standing in front of a carriage.

"To be honest, we don't know how many nights we're going to stay," said Julia. I was moving closer to the counter now. Dona Adiles looked at her without speaking. "I mean, two, I think. But is it okay if we decide to stay longer?"

"Fine."

And she took the registration sheet from Julia's hand.

Through the window, I could see some of the cabins and the little stone paths leading to up them. The others sat in a dip in the ground and only their roofs were visible from reception.

"Can we choose our cabin?" I asked. "We'd prefer one at the back." And I smiled at Julia.

The woman shrugged.

"They're all the same."

• • •

The entire time Julia lived in Porto Alegre, she had stayed at that all-girls residence. Decent girls who believed in God and cooked instant pasta under the fluorescent lights of the large communal kitchen. Girls who, every Friday, would pack their suitcase before going to class, come back, shower, change clothes, lock the doors, take the stairs as fast as the sisters in charge would allow, then raise their arms in the middle of the congested street and share a cab to the coach station. Sometimes, before boarding the intercity coach, each heading for the only town she really knew, they would sit together on the high stools in the snack bar for some fried chicken and a juice, not liking one bit the way the men looked at them.

Julia would sleep for the entire journey, only waking after passing under the familiar arch at the entrance to the town, eyes turning towards the parking lot, and of course her father's black car would be there waiting for her. Some time after midnight. A hug, a kiss. During the five-minute journey through the dead streets to her family home, the two of them would exchange very few words.

Soledade was small and, by night, even smaller.

Seemingly, the disadvantage of growing up in the interior is that you, or your parents, might be the topic of discussion in every well-lighted dining room within a three-mile radius. That's why it's best not to provide any ammunition to fuel the gossip, or at least that was what Julia used to say when I asked her what it had been like to spend her entire adolescence in a place of that size. I was interested in the deviations: someone who's bored ends up doing stupid things, that was my belief and arguably my way of life, but apparently there was no deviation at all in Julia, a regular life with a regular family: the mother, one of the last housewives I'd come across, a father who measured social ascent by the size of his garage, a brother whose future wife happened, not by chance, to be his childhood sweetheart.

By the end of the day on Sunday, Julia would be on her way back to Porto Alegre and ready for class and the group work that she did for the whole group. Sitting on her bed in the residence, she would open her books and write, while into her room filtered the sounds of girls playing cards in a common room with a crucifix and a disfigured Jesus, a threadbare rug, an armchair with tapered legs that someone had left there out of charity or gratitude, as well as the eight-seat table on the side of which was written *ass*. Julia stayed in her room doing her work, even though the journalism department wasn't quite as demanding as her dedication would suggest. But she had become accustomed to being a responsible, sometimes brilliant student, effectively ever since the point where they started encouraging competition between children at school. And being in Porto Alegre at the age of eighteen, without her family, practically without friends, living in a residence where she had to follow strict rules of cohabitation, didn't seem to intimidate her at all.

I waited a while before approaching her. The truth was that, to begin with, I wasn't very interested at all. There was something that made me turn up my nose at that girl from the interior. I think she had the air of those people who feel prematurely proud of the brilliant future they imagine for themselves. And that attitude also seemed to assert that Julia's present existence was nothing more than a wait, as tedious as it was inevitable. There weren't even many opportunities to prove myself wrong, if that were the case, because every Friday she took the damned coach to the Capital of Precious Stones. Her mom was a good cook, although no one had ever asked whether she enjoyed it, Mathias was going to marry his long-term girlfriend, Julia helped her dad pack amethysts in plastic bubble wrap. Some of her old friends were studying in Passo Fundo, others had stayed put, spending Saturday mornings negotiating with impoverished mineral prospectors, then later on showing foreign entrepreneurs to their families' stores for them to examine macaws and obelisks and trees sculpted out of precious stone while they tried sips of maté, pulling faces and laughing at themselves.

When Julia and I actually spoke for the first time it was at a costume party. She was dressed as Penelope Pitstop, I was a punk heroin addict. My outfit included a syringe without the needle, which I carried in my pocket with the plunger sticking out. At that costume party, during our first semester in the media department, I met her waiting in line at the bar and her mere presence at that event was enough to surprise me. If you'd asked me to pick words that defined Julia Ceratti out of a basket full of them, I'd look for *normal* or *serious* or *dedicated*. She was the girl who raised her hand to ask a question with five minutes to go before the end of class.

And yet it just happened, we began to trade impressions of that warehouse full of people, where a samba school with a strange name used to rehearse, but which was now invaded by middle-class university students who were increasingly drunk, euphoric and self-centered. Some of them would spend the whole night trying to explain to everyone else what on earth they were dressed as. That girl there, for example, what's that on her head? Julia was laughing deliciously, even though she averted her eyes from mine at times, as though she were looking for something better to do. When it was her turn to be served, she tugged a screwed up banknote out of her pocket. She barely waited for her change. Using the hand with which she clutched her can of beer, she began to push her way through the crowd and advanced a fair distance before remembering I was there and turning back. "I always wanted to talk to you, Cora." She said this categorically, with no interest in any possible response, and then she disappeared.

It was rather odd, yes, but I didn't want to give myself a headache over it, so I returned to the corner where my friends were, Alex from *Clockwork Orange*, a surgeon, a flapper in a very short skirt, a guy with a vampire cloak who had just tossed his plastic canine teeth in the trash. They were rating the teachers, making conjectures that weren't particularly funny or deep about their private lives. Beyond the general comments about the teaching staff, coursework, the dilapidated media building, the lousy food in the university canteen, none of us had much to say to one another, when it came down to it.

By about five in the morning most people had left. The sound reverberated around the empty corners of the warehouse, leaving a metallic sensation in my ears that seemed irreversible. Not many of the girls could be bothered dancing any more, and those who could seemed to be doing it in order to impress someone who almost certainly was no longer there. Of my acquaintances, only Alex remained, his eye half lined with mascara, in a solitary and contemplative state. A pink panther was looking for its own tail. There was no more beer for sale. Just *caipirinha* and cheap whiskey.

I decided to leave too. I went up to Alex and shouted that I was going. He raised his hand slightly, in a gesture that vaguely resembled a bye. I said: "You're going to catch a cab?" He babbled something. I left the party.

There was a line of taxis on Avenida Ipiranga. The driver of the first kept shouting taxi, taxi, taxi. It was quite an old car with its door open, and the reclined driver's seat made me think of someone sunbathing in a lounger at the beach. I turned to the side. Julia was there. She had sat down on a low wall. Her Penelope Pitstop gloves lay in her lap. She kept running her fingertips over the satin. She seemed like someone with a lot of problems.

"I think I got left behind," she said when I approached. "Our classmate from Sobradinho went home. Do you know our classmate from Sobradinho?"

"Yes."

"Where do you live, Cora?"

"Petrópolis. And you?"

"Maria Imaculada Residence." She laughed as if slightly sorry for herself. "The sisters wouldn't like you with those pants of yours and that ripped blouse."

"That's fine. I don't have much love for them either."

She thought about it.

"Sure. You'd think my dad could rent an apartment for me here, wouldn't you? Pfff. Of course he could. He rents one for my brother in Passo Fundo, and my brother is the kind of guy who knows how long it takes for dirty dishes to get moldy. But hey, my parents want the sisters to keep an eye on me."

"You're not planning to go back to the residence, what's it called?"

"Maria Imaculada."

"You're not planning to go back to the Maria Imaculada just now, are you?"

"Pretty much. I'm trying to come up with a better plan."

"Can't you just not turn up for a night?"

"The sisters will snitch on me. They'll call Soledade and say, 'Your daughter went out at 11 at night and still . . .'"

"Okay. Let me think. When the sisters call Soledade, your parents will find out that you just did the most innocent thing in the world, stayed over at a friend's house after a party, see? I can speak to them if you like."

"Where exactly do you live?"

"Petrópolis."

"I've never been to Petrópolis. Is it a house?"

"Yes, a house."

She stood up.

"It seems you're a lucky girl, Cora."

I was still lying in bed, tossing from side to side. Surrounded by wooden planks and cheap prints and all that space outside. Julia had gone round the back of the cabin to ask for help riding a horse, the most docile, an old mare, because she hadn't ridden for years and she was a bit scared. It was me who had suggested she call the blue-eyed farmhand. She didn't say yes or no, but soon banged the door and so I lay there a few moments more, thinking about the little we had seen and what was still to come.

The room was shady and a light, cool breeze came through the slightly open window, making the small net curtain sway. No voices, not a single sign of human life outside. In my entire life, I had never ridden a horse. I prefer to avoid situations that make me look like an idiot, so I said: "That farmhand must be crazy to help you." He was the owner's grandson. And Julia slammed the door and went off to find him.

I yawned, then rolled onto the opposite side of the bed, where the sheet and bedspread, perfectly smooth, seemed to want to disguise the fact that someone had slept there. On the nightstand, next to a common black ashtray, Julia had left her turquoise Navajo bracelet.

There was no doubt it was a beautiful bracelet. Two feathers engraved in silver, the bright blue lozenge between them. It had been made at an indigenous reserve in Arizona. It had been purchased from a silent Native American at that same reserve, back when Julia and Eric were happy. I put on the bracelet and got out of bed. Without my realizing it, the room had become lighter, a sign that the sun was momentarily free of clouds. I began to look for my checkered shirt. Our cases were open, and Julia had spread out her multiple bags of make-up and useless creams over the table. There was also a bit of wheat bran. Half a salami that should have been kept in a cool place. Two unopened bottles of wine. There was my shirt, screwed up on a chair, so I put it on and buttoned it from bottom to top. Then I opened the closet, where there was a good-sized mirror. For quite a while I just looked at myself like that, shirt, panties, bracelet. It gave me a strange pleasure.

Since the previous day, there had been a new element in the story, and he was called Eric Aslan.

"Eric isn't Muslim," Julia had said. We were heading towards town. The car rocked about in the ruts of the dirt road.

"You know, lots of people get that wrong."

"I didn't say anything about him being Muslim."

"I know, Cora."

The car jolted suddenly to the left. Julia laughed.

"After all, Eric eats sausages. He loves sausages."

"Does he know you're here?"

"Not precisely here," she replied, gesturing the landscape with her index finger. Small properties were scattered on both sides of the track. Wooden barns or shelters for firewood, vineyards, houses with well-tended gardens, others with fading walls that suggested some years of neglect, on the verandas of which there was always a puppy curled up like a Swiss roll, barely raising its head when the car passed.

Eric had grown up in a suburb of west Boston. Picture a lot of oversized houses, some with games rooms and greenhouses, with water automatically sprinkling over the well-trimmed lawns in the late afternoon. That was the Aslans' American dream. But, after 9/11, it wasn't uncommon for the neighbors to get confused and imagine an open Koran on the coffee table in the living room. Only that they weren't even Arabs. Turks and Arabs were as different as a Navajo Indian and a Guarani Indian. But what did it matter when Eric insisted on sporting that thick beard? If that wasn't enough, the word Aslan sounded dangerously close to Islam.

One day, Eric got tired of having to explain. The worst thing was when people shot glances at him in the street and he wasn't able to defend himself. When the time came, he decided on a university beyond the border. The Americans of Massachusetts were close enough to the province of Quebec to have an opinion on it, but far enough away for that opinion to be quite wrong; to them, that place might as well have been France: a strange world with elastic rules. Eric liked that. So much so that what attracted him most in the beginning, before setting foot in Montreal and meeting Julia in a certain class and then sharing a room with her in a house full of foreign students, was the fact that he only had to be eighteen in order to drink any kind of alcoholic drink imaginable. Eighteen, not twenty-one. Which gave him three extra years of partying.

When she had finished telling me about Eric, Julia turned to face me as if it were my turn to speak, but I didn't know what to say. I wasn't remotely surprised. Julia dating an American seemed rather predictable, to tell the truth. Nor was it unexpected that she felt proud of the fact. Which was kind of funny, and proved that there was, in that regard at least, a vast difference between us. In Paris, I only hooked up with people who were as uprooted as I was, peripheral citizens who felt rather uncomfortable at suddenly finding themselves at the center of everything, dazzled by beauty, confused by manners, numb with cold, and sick and tired of appetizer-entrée-dessert and the mechanical exchanges of niceties. So I said nothing to Julia, I just kept driving. Luckily, after a few moments of awkwardness, she asked me to stop. We had reached a colonial house that was falling to pieces. Julia got out of the car and crouched in the middle of the road to take some photos. The sun was strong and at times she held her hand over the viewfinder in order to block the light and see how the photos were turning out. I got out too. She climbed a couple of stairs and tried to peer through the ruined door.

"Maybe I'm done with Eric," she said, still spying through a crack that seemed more likely to have been caused by man than by the years passing. "Like, you know, this is another time. I've changed."

Now I was surprised.

"The boxes," I said, suddenly recalling our conversation on Skype.

"Yes. The boxes."

The reunion. The suggestion of a trip. Now it all seemed more logical.

"Tell me something, does this Eric know about me?"

"In what way?" She laughed. "Yes, I think I mentioned you to him once or twice."

We got back in the car.

Something told me that Eric was sitting at a window at that precise moment, guessing at the outline of snow-covered things while he dreamed about the paradise beach where Julia would supposedly meet her parents. No, he didn't know that she was here. Definitely not that she was with me.

When Julia returned to the cabin, I was still in front of the mirror. Check shirt, panties, bracelet. She walked past me and said: "looking hot." Then she went into the bathroom as if she were in a hurry. She wasn't covered in dirt nor had she broken a bone, so I assumed that the horse had been good for her. I put the Navajo bracelet back in its place. As I dressed, Julia spoke at length about how excellent horse riding was, a pity I hadn't tried it. The reverberation on the tiles increased the strength of her voice. Her story took a good few minutes. Towards the end, I went over to the bathroom and, leaning on the doorframe, said:

"Good thing you didn't get hurt."

She turned on the faucet.

"Since when have you been scared about that?"

Julia was drying her hands when something beeped in the bedroom. She left the bathroom and I looked at myself in the mirror, which was the same as looking at her, in the background, looking for her bag, then finding her bag and looking for her cell inside it, then looking at the screen, and finally saying "message from Eric," still looking, longer than it would usually take to look at a damn text message.

I hadn't taken a phone with me, although my mom had repeatedly insisted that I take hers. After all, she barely left the house now, while I would be spending who knew how many weeks in what she exaggeratedly referred to as a "risky situation." I couldn't help laughing. I said: "Mom, relax. Nothing's going to happen to me." She saw me off with the promise that, at least occasionally, I would make some kind of contact. Neither of us mentioned my dad. And my mother started waving, in the middle of the street where I grew up, until the car had completely disappeared.

Julia and I were sitting in the square in the town center (my mom didn't like Julia). Around us was a handful of historic houses. The leaflets from the Antônio Prado Tourist Bureau said that this was the most Italian place in Brazil. Forty-eight colonial wooden houses sitting within the municipal boundaries, lots of polenta on the menu, lots of rambling tales from grandparents speaking a dialect imprisoned by time. The people who arrived with empty stomachs from the Veneto valley had filled those stomachs in this part of Rio Grande do Sul, where, in the mid 1900s, there was still space. At school, the teachers told how the German immigrants had kept the good part of the highlands, and the Italians were left with the stony soil of the foothills. It didn't seem too bad now.

"Tell me about Paris," Julia said suddenly.

I thought about it. So I told her that I lived in the Chinese quarter. That my apartment was a hundred and sixty square feet and had a single window. That in the afternoon I made sandwiches near Notre-Dame for tourists who weren't particularly interested in trying the local cuisine.

Julia made herself comfortable on the bench.

"You're doing a fashion course, a fashion course in Paris. You're not going to make it sound ugly and hard, Cora, sorry."

"Tell me something about your life in Montreal."

"If you throw a bucket of water out of the window in December, it freezes in mid-air."

Looking around the square, some of the buildings made no contribution whatsoever to the vaguely turn-of-the-century feel that others, collapsing or restored, uselessly tried to recreate. A lottery kiosk, three stories of reflective glass or the glittering biblical scene next to the mother church. Generally, I had the impression that, as soon as the economic situation allowed, the families of Antônio Prado, supposedly proud of their origins, would drop everything and head for the nearest hardware store, choosing to cover everything in shiny hard surfaces in the belief that they were much more modern and practical.

Julia was biting her cuticles, her gaze lost on the children playing on the other side of the square. Since Eric had made contact, I hadn't left her side. I knew, therefore, that the message had received no response.

"Hey, aren't you going to reply to Eric?"

She stretched out her arms and pulled a face as if she had back pain.

"I don't know. Are you worried about it?"

"No. Just wanted to know."

Julia seemed to have found something about my question funny. Perhaps she wasn't thinking about Eric, or the message itself and whether to reply, but about my funny question. I think that made me want to offer a lengthy explanation. I had that foible sometimes. I started to say that I had developed a theory relating to cell phones, and she asked what theory, to which I replied that we needed to free ourselves of them as soon as possible, I couldn't remember whether that was in our initial plans, and anyway, our plans had been made so long ago, technologically speaking, but the fact was that cell phones or any kind of communication with the outside world weren't in keeping with the spirit of our libertarian pilgrimage. I added that last bit to make her laugh.

She said she'd think about it, laughing.

"You won't think about it."

"I will! Promise."

We exchanged a smile and then we dropped the subject.

That second day in Antônio Prado, Julia and I walked up and down. We climbed flights of stairs to high neighborhoods with houses new and old, where elderly ladies sat at windows watching the street and their own backyard and waited for the flowers to bloom. Young men drove around aimlessly in cars. I think it's safe to say that their idea of youth consisted largely of aerodynamics, shiny hubcaps and huge sound systems in their trunks. I wondered where the girls were, where the hell the single girls of that city were, and how the owners of those cars went about meeting such reserved young ladies. It wasn't easy growing up in a place where you had to put all your energy into customizing a motor vehicle or, in the case of the girls, into anything that was contained within four walls and was necessarily supervised by a responsible adult. To make things worse, there were so many churches, so many saint someone-or-others, and probably just as many promises of virginity.

I thought about all of this, but I didn't dare make any comments of a religious nature in front of Julia. She was wearing a pendant round her neck right now. I had caught sight of the little Jesus or saint when she changed clothes in the cabin because of a greasy stain. She took off her denim jacket, then her blouse. She also changed her pants because the ones she was wearing didn't go with the new top half. Then I saw the oval pendant, and you know that those kinds of pendants don't show Elvis Presleys or Kurt Cobains, they are Catholic memorabilia, pure and simple. I had seen other things too: matching bra and panties with thin bands of black lace, maybe an extra six or seven pounds accentuating the thighs, the pale skin of a winter spent in the northern hemisphere. "Pass me that t-shirt," she said, pointing at the open suitcase. "Right on top." I reached for the t-shirt and left everything else where it was.

Late that afternoon, when we stopped at an ice cream parlor after a lot of walking, Julia unfolded our map of Rio Grande do Sul. It was the size of the table. She was studying it as if she was going to be tested on it. As for me, I started on the strawberry ice cream, searching for the chocolate so that I could mix them on the same spoonful. There was no one but us in the parlor, except for the server. She was doing Sudoku behind the cash register.

"Have you been to many of these places?" Julia asked.

I took a swig of water.

"Hmm, almost none."

I could see the chain that would lead to that little saint. The almost imperceptible silver links around the neck, which descended carelessly among her freckles until they disappeared. Julia raised her eyes from the map.

"That's because your mom and dad kept taking you to medieval castles when you were little."

"That's it. Goddamn aristocrats."

"Oh, stop it, it must have been fun to find out about the Middle Ages. Did you see those little openings where they used to pour out hot oil?"

"I did."

"Wow. And what else?"

"A whole load of tapestries."

She smiled and looked at the map again. My feet were throbbing, I put them up on a chair, which made a certain amount of unintentional noise, causing the server to interrupt her intermediate level Sudoku, turn in my direction and recriminate me with thoughts that were as clear as the speech bubbles in comic strips. I pretended it had nothing to do with me, my feet were throbbing after all. You'd think those boots would be comfortable, because once upon a time something very similar clad the feet of soldiers who had to eat tinned food and walk all day on snowy fields, through forests under surveillance, finding body parts on the path, but not at all, the boots were just another problem. Julia started to laugh. "What is it?" I asked, to which she replied: "Look, there's a city here in Rio Grande do Sul called Formigueiro and another called Suspiro.

Anthill and Sigh." Then we started reading out all the absurd names we found, which was slightly more difficult for me as I had to read everything upside down, and so Julia and I made fun of the small towns of Restinga Seca, São João do Polesine, Faxinal do Soturno, Chuvisca, Trigolândia, Anta Gorda, Tio Hugo, Não-Me-Toque, Boa Vista do Cadeado, Mormaço, Espumoso, the last two of which weren't very far from Sole-dade, which as it happens was a rather unusual name too. Among the many laughs of that hour in the ice cream parlor, which I would venture to say had become the most uninhib-ited moment of our reunion so far, Julia told me that her dad had lived for three years in Espumoso before marrying, and perhaps there was no reason for me to suspect that that state-ment put an end to our game, the funny names would always have run out anyway, but the fact was that soon afterwards Julia leaned back abruptly as if she wanted to free herself once and for all from that map, and then she sighed heavily. I could hear the hum of the freezers as she sat perfectly still. Then, very slowly, she stretched out her arm for her sundae glass, which was more or less on the border with Uruguay, but all that re-mained in it was a creamy pool of an indeterminate color. She gave up. I wanted to understand why Julia's mood sometimes changed so suddenly. She had always been that way.

I folded the map and paid for the two ice creams. Outside, the sun was just about touching the roofs of the most faraway houses, and the warm light exploded on the rectangular paving stones. When we started walking, Julia said, as if continuing a very serious conversation I couldn't recall at all: "It's great that my parents are happy at the beach." We crossed the road and I asked what she actually meant. So she gave the kind of laugh used to apologize preemptively, a pretty little laugh that tends to suffocate any counter-argument, and said that the fact that her parents no longer lived in Soledade seemed, to her eyes, more of an abrupt rupture between her and her native town than her own departure for Canada. I had no time to ask whether that wasn't rather unfair because she immediately continued saying that, to make the situation worse, Mathias had moved to a place a couple of miles from Soledade, he was an agronomist and looked after two or three soya plantations that obviously didn't belong to him, but to very rich people who didn't actually understand soya at all, concluding: "You're lucky to be an only child," and without taking a breath: "It must be much easier that way."

That was what Julia said before we got into the car. I'm an only child, I thought. I'm an only child, and never in my entire life did I ask for a sibling.

3.

THE BLUE-EYED FARMHAND had shown Julia a small dirt road that didn't appear on the map. The following day, nice and early, we left Antônio Prado on that road. It ran along the edge of a precipice and we caught glimpses, down at the bottom, amid the foothills of the bushy mountains, of the various twists and turns of the River Antas. Country music was playing on the stereo. Nasal vocals, guitar, some mention of Tennessee. Julia was happy, as was I, of course, although I was gripping on tightly to the steering wheel and my tires kept encroaching on the opposite lane (where, luckily, there was nothing coming), just like an old lady undertaking the arduous task of going home. All of this was justified by my fear of heights, although that didn't make me like the place any less; there was no doubt that it was a very scenic route and that the best way to get someplace, the next place, could only be this, with mist scudding across the mountain tops, the fresh air, the pines, a few vineyards, Julia, the quietness. And then, suddenly, without the farmhand having mentioned it, a tiny chapel about a hundred years old. The nave was being cleaned. A dozen or so wicker chairs had been piled up outside.

As far as I could remember, I had never been able to visualize the landscapes, the people and the situations our trip would entail, even having given it a lot of thought. I'm not talking about specific things like that little chapel, which I doubt many people knew about, except for the locals, or the way the light falls on the hills between Antônio Prado and São Marcos, I mean any vague idea, which might be completely wrong, or even fall into the most banal of stereotypes. Something, basically, to fill up space and time. Was it because I lacked points of reference, having been raised in Porto Alegre with no aunts, uncles, grandparents or cousins to visit in the interior? I don't believe that was the case. The thing was that our idea always had the appearance of a long line stretching between nothing and nothing. I mean, I honestly didn't know whether Julia thought that way. I did. As for her, she might have always been interested in picturesque cottages. How could I be sure that what was important for Julia, as for me, wasn't being in a certain place, but getting out of another?

The track came out in a cobbled street in São Marcos. It seemed like a fairly ordinary town, so we passed through without paying much attention, occasionally pulling up to the curb, lowering the window, giving a toothy grin and asking how to get to Mulada. São Jorge da Mulada, in the rural belt. We had to do this three times before getting it right. Then the shutters started to come down, the shop signs, the villas, the electricity poles overloaded with cables all disappeared, and as the velvety folds of curtain were raised into the rigging, a gently undulating field, more burnt ochre than any nuance of green, with araucarias scattered here and there, appeared surprisingly in front of us.

It was called Campos de Cima da Serra and, in the eighteenth century, troops and their contraband mules from Uruguay had gone there. After slogging for months and months in a country that was barely born, experiencing attacks from Indians, hunger, illness, storms, they arrived in the middle of Brazil and sold their mules for the price of gold. A mule, what was it again? A cross between a donkey and a mare. One of those, at that time, could be worth something like forty cows because they played a vital role in mining, out there in the depths of Minas Gerais. The farmhand had told Julia all this while I was busy with something else.

Now she was looking out of the window, resting her head against it. I think she had gotten tired of the precise view offered by the front windshield. She wanted to see the landscape moving quickly.

"Are we looking for something specific?" I asked.

Her voice mingled with the wind.

"Not one thing. Several."

"That the blue-eyed farmhand told you about?"

"Wanna stop this business of calling the guy a farmhand?"

"Okay, fine. But what did he tell you?"

Suddenly, some kind of unusual monument appeared on the horizon, with a spire pointing skywards, staircases and two silhouettes that seemed to be human.

Julia smiled, pleased at this unexpected chain of events.

"This was one of the things he told me about."

It was no exaggeration to say that this memorial turned out to be without doubt the strangest, most out-of-place thing I saw on the entire journey. Someone ill-informed, on seeing the general whiteness of the construction, the straightness of the lines, the bronze statues on a rectangular base, might even have been convinced that it was a tomb to the unknown soldier, but they would only have to move closer to those statues for that surefire military hypothesis to unravel. Two men with accordions? In any case, we didn't have a war behind us, or rather, there were many wars, none which was particularly clear, documented, told, and retold, for us to then go erecting pieces of concrete and crying for all those who fell. No cemeteries of white crosses. No blockbuster movies. No tears for strangers. Our men ended up being flattened in the middle of the countryside, and it was the wind that fluttered their red neckerchiefs, that took away their horses and left their women in a state of panic, that entered open mouths and abandoned ranches and made the branches of an *umbu* tree burst into flames, that witnessed a stone fall in the ruins of Sete Povos das Missões and even led the Indians to believe in the fire serpent Boitatá, and that's why they closed their eyes so tightly.

This was what had happened in the place where I was born. You can read about such courageous people in historical novels, but sometimes they're not entirely truthful. That monument, anyway, did not pay homage to any soldier or revolution, even though the language had something rather grandiose and consequently ridiculous about it. In beautiful metal letters: TO THE BERTUSSI BROTHERS, FROM THE GAUCHO HOMELAND. Their names were Honeyde and Adelar, and the apex of their heroism, according to an illustrated timeline, had been to introduce drums into the regional music. Both wore typical gaucho clothing, boots, *bombachas*, shirt, neckerchief. The younger-looking one, in so far as you can compare two bronze statues, held his accordion to his shoulders, fingers hovering over the keyboard and the buttons on the opposite side. As for the older of the two, he was immortalized in a rather comical pose, with one hand on his hip (as if suffering from lower back pain) and the right leg supported on his accordion (which surely showed a certain lack of respect for the instrument?).

Julia began to laugh, in the middle of the memorial site.

"All this for the Bertussis, I can't believe it."

"You've heard of these guys?"

"My uncle Francisco played accordion when I was little."

Given that Julia had grown up in Soledade, that didn't seem strange at all. To me, however, gaucho music was as far removed as celtic songs or aboriginal drums. I seemed to recall one single memory, very vague and hazy, involving accordions, traditional frocks, and formally dressed gauchos jumping around a sword without stepping on it. It was at a steak house in Porto Alegre, which, in addition to food, offered customers a full folkloric show. So full that my parents decided to leave before the show finished.

"Have you never heard *Oh de casa*?"

I shook my head.

"My uncle used to play it for me."

Then she pretended she was holding an accordion to her chest, her hands opening and closing the squeeze-box as she fingered invisible keys, her feet joining in the choreography, one of them lifting a couple of inches off the floor, then the other, but the most impressive thing was that Julia was singing. She knew the lyrics by heart. Her voice was deeper than usual. The r's much more rolled.

I come from far away with a long path still to tread,
I beg of you, kind sir, for a place to lay my head.
Bring your boy and dismount, put the horse in the stable,
In this ranch there's a bed and hot food on the table.

I think I felt rather disconcerted after Julia's performance. I started trying to follow the Bertussi brothers' timeline, like someone who lacks the patience to read long texts on museum walls, but who doesn't feel right being defeated by them. In truth, I was looking at the photographs. Only the photographs. In one of them, Adelar Bertussi, with his inseparable accordion, was holding out an enormous gourd of maté. Did old uncle Francisco perhaps resemble him slightly? Did Adelar dye his beard? And, if so, why not the rest of his hair as well? Was Julia's uncle by any chance gray haired? Why did he no longer play the accordion?

The strange thing was that I had never met a single wretched member of her family. Although her father went to Porto Alegre frequently, supposedly on business, we had never been introduced to one another. On one of those occasions, I was convinced that Julia was doing everything she could to avoid the encounter, like someone sending you out the back door to greet someone else at the front. That, of course, is a manner of speaking. Everything seemed to be timed, basically, so that we wouldn't meet. The same with Mathias, who went to the city now and then, and that's probably not counting the other times I didn't even know about. Back then, I was intrigued by everything about her. I really wanted to get to know the Cerattis. I wanted them to tell me stories about her childhood, and for Julia to be mortified and try to change the subject. And what about Soledade? I'd always wanted to see Soledade. We were sufficiently close for Julia to have made the invitation, but she hadn't even come close to that.

I soon got bored of the timeline. I looked around me. Julia was at the other side of the memorial. Elbows on the railings, leaning slightly forward, she seemed to be concentrating hard on the stillness of a little red house. There were some cows nearby, and a small weir. Julia tucked a few strands of hair behind her ear. Sometimes, all of a sudden, it became difficult to reconcile that person, the contemplative-depressive, with the other, a thousand miles an hour, private shows in the middle of nowhere, double life in the capital at eighteen, Montreal and the world at twenty-one. Perhaps I was in love again and, worse, without the slightest idea what my chances were. I mean, there was a chance (in the sense of it having happened before). And yet there wasn't (in the sense that it ended badly).

Julia turned back.

I shouted: "Shall we go?"

And so we returned to the car in silence.

Yes, I was attracted to girls. Technically, I was bisexual. My own timeline would show all the signs. Played with Ninja Turtles. Went to soccer camp. Refused to wear a skirt. Fell in love with female teachers. Enjoyed a sci-fi series whose female villain was actually a lizard and yet utterly tempting. Wanted to talk about it and fell for the female psychologist. Went to gay clubs with a fake ID. Watched the clip of Alicia Silverstone and Liv Tyler running wild on the road two hundred times, and alone, and lying face down. Kissed classmates in public restrooms. Wrote feminist phrases on ripped jeans. Was a fan of rock bands fronted by women. Stopped the car on a dark road and jumped into the back seat with Marina, then with Luciana, then with Amanda. Read *Lolita*. Read the complete works of Hilda Hilst. Got some girl's number and she never answered. Saw *Wild Things*, kept rewinding to the pool scene. Lied she was at a friend's house when it was a motel whose décor was supposed to resemble a dungeon. If you turned off the right lights, it could more or less have been one.

But I said *bisexual*. Girls and some guys. Or, to be more exact: guy. Girl. Girl. Girl. Guy. Girl. Girl. Guy. And that tended to be the ratio from then on. I went with guys out of inertia. Girls, out of fascination. With guys, everything took place as if in the script of a rom-com for the general public (except that I was just faking the role I'd been given). With girls, everything began, continued and ended with the purest melodrama. First boy: at fourteen, after a Carnival dance in Tramandaí, day was breaking as he sat on the edge of the bed to put his shirt on. First girl: at fifteen, she seemed confused, she asked if I'd done this before, I lied that I had, and she said, "You can tell." Boys asked me out, I was pretty, perhaps rather mysterious to them, I didn't ask them to call me afterwards. With girls I had to battle, inch by inch, a hand resting on a thigh, an exchange of glances, then finally a kiss. Sometimes I had to convince them that they wanted to be with me. I'm saying this because it wasn't uncommon for me to fall for a straight girl. Perhaps that has been my greatest mistake: I never accepted the fact that I couldn't want just *anyone*, but ideally only those who existed within the four walls of a place called gay. For God's sake, I wanted to fall in love with the next girl to walk along the street and be in with a chance. Not be afraid of getting involved with someone who might wake up the next day and regret it. But I ended up being a lapse for many people. A quickly outgrown phase for others. My attraction to the female sex was both a sweet adventure and a condemnation to the most claustrophobic of worlds.

The worst part, without doubt, was having to face my parents. It had been a long time since I'd given up on serious conversations with them. You know how it is, they vote for the left and are all for human rights and minorities until you show up at home with your girlfriend. Then the first thing they say is that they have no problem whatsoever accepting your "choices," but that the rest of society, unfortunately, will stigmatize them. And, after all, they're only looking out for your best interests. They love the word stigmatize, but of course it's always other people who are responsible for that unfortunate error of judgment.

And that's not all. Are you going to miss out on the wonderful opportunity to have a child? Will you deny your child the chance to grow up at the heart of a normal family? That was the kind of thing they'd have said, if the conversation had ever taken place. But in truth there wasn't even time for that kind of conversation. When my parents separated, I was sixteen. The most famous otorhinolaryngologist in Porto Alegre contented himself, from that moment on, with the following parental obligations: two meet-ups a week, Wednesdays and Sundays, during which we spent more time chewing frozen food than trying to create any kind of complicity. Therefore it was my mother I needed to deceive on a daily basis. Through our house passed a never-ending parade of "best friends"; if one vanished with no explanation, there was soon another crossing the living room in socks to get a glass of water from the kitchen. Where had the two of us met? This was always rather vague. And my mom, although all the signs were available to her without her even having to leave the house, had decided to avoid confrontation. For a while, at least.

Then, one sleepy afternoon, she opened my bedroom door. She wouldn't have been able to explain why, she always knocked, whether I had company or not, that was a rule she liked to stick to. That afternoon, however, with some excuse at the tip of her tongue, my mom entered my room entirely unexpectedly, perhaps wanting more than anything to employ some stupid pretext, something like: do you need anything? I'm going out, isn't today the day to pick up your jacket from the dry cleaner? What she saw, however, in that bedroom full of icons she didn't understand, made her shut the door in a split second and run downstairs in search of the telephone. She dialed her ex-husband. Somewhat stunned, she had the delicacy to go through the habitual niceties while she searched for a way to describe the scene, your daughter's friend lying on the bed, panties with an almost childlike print, your daughter with her hand in—her hand in those panties, I always knew Cora would do something like this.

Following my embarrassment at being caught in flagrante, my mom and I cried in separate rooms for several weeks. My tears were squeezed between my cheeks and two soft layers of pillow, for me and me alone. As for my mother's waterworks, they seemed to be a mere detail in a whole pyrotechnic display of Greek tragedy, as if the distance between actress (her) and audience (me) meant her whole body had to show the fact that she was sobbing, with puffs and trembles and hisses and sighs and objects that fell from their places, for example, a glass duck from Murano, bound installments of *Cooking from A to Z*, a ceramic pot that had always been the sugar pot, the only picture frame holding a photo of my maternal grandparents.

I can remember, it was May. As always in May, winter had already appropriated the nights to have a bit of a rehearsal. I put on a hoodie over my pajama and went out into the garden, clutching a cup of peppermint tea. My mom didn't follow. Before our family crisis, I didn't tend to go to that part of the house. There was a Parisian-style iron bench, next to a rose bush that was always in bloom, but I think the last time it was used was for tying up helium balloons on one of my birthdays. I sat on that bench and stared at the street.

Ours was essentially a residential street, dominated by two story houses from the seventies, like ours. I had never lived anywhere else. Near the corner, there was a wooden sentry box, where there was a guard, paid for by the homeowners on the block. The guard that year was called Leônidas. At that time, he must have been about the age I am now, no more than twenty-six and no less than twenty-two, but when you're a teenager you don't tend to think of people in that age group as young; on the contrary, we find it only natural for them to be teaching us biology or Portuguese, treating our broken arm, selling us a guitar; they seem so distant, after all, so secure, so adult, and only when we reach that age do we realize that the abyss wasn't insurmountable, that there wasn't even an abyss, that it was only details that separated us, maybe slightly more in Leônidas's case, as his guard's salary went to raising two children, photos of whom were pulled from his wallet whenever he got chatting.

On those terrible May nights, I sat in the garden, thinking that it wasn't fair of my mom to cast me in the role of villain. Couldn't she spare me the daily demonstrations of her suffering? I warmed my hands on the teacup. Leônidas had to take a turn around the whole block and he would always pass me, on the other side of the fence. "Hi Cora." Or : "Evening, Cora." I think, at that time, it must have been obvious that something wasn't right in our little family nucleus, and Leônidas might have suspected why. He had only to look at me with a bit of scrutiny. At sixteen, I was already what you used to call a tomboy. Put it this way, aunts and great aunts loved pulling me into a corner to suggest drastic changes to my appearance, after all I'd look so good with a patterned dress and some sandals, and why didn't I wear my hair loose? Loose hair would only enhance the delicate contours of my face.

Leônidas used to look at me properly, especially on those nights, but the only thing he ever dared say was: "Aren't you cold, honey?" Always the same question.

I would reply with a friendly chuckle. When I got tired of doing nothing in the garden, I went to my room to watch television.

But, as the year progressed, the situation in my house gradually improved, until we returned to the level of accord we'd enjoyed before I was caught in the act. My mom continued asking where I went, and I continued telling the truth only when it was in my interests, that is, on the occasions when my nighttime activities involved someone male. In January, I did the university entrance exam. I got a place to study journalism. A banner was hung on our balcony. WELL DONE, CORA! 8TH IN JOURNALISM—UNIVERSIDADE FEDERAL.

My dad, whenever he had the chance, went into a bookshop and came out with some great work wrapped up as a gift, Truman Capote, Norman Mailer, Tom Wolfe, because at some dinner I had mentioned the words *literary journalism*, and luckily there was a whole collection of books under that name. By the time classes actually began, I already loved the profession enough to be immune to the disappointments. I made more friends in one semester than in eleven years at school. My appearance began to transform, especially after I read *The Empire of Fashion*, by Gilles Lipovetsky, for communication theory. It wasn't the change my aunts expected, of course. For example, I turned some old jeans into very short shorts. I did let my hair hang loose, then I cut it and put a ring in my nose. I liked the idea of becoming more attractive and, to my personal understanding of fashion psychology, that didn't mean becoming more feminine. On the contrary, I tended to reject anything contaminated by concepts of fragility or an excess of fluff, like bows, polka dots, lace, dolly shoes, gold accessories, heart patterns. None of that had anything to do with me.

So Julia and I became friends and started going around together and more or less forgot about the rest of our classmates, but I had no idea how much she knew about me. I mean, about my sexuality. At that time, I was dating a girl call Amanda, a physical education major, nearly five feet eleven, who drizzled a thin trail of ketchup on each French fry instead of making a red pool with it. That made me uncomfortable. I had told some people I barely knew about Amanda. In the media department, everyone was very committed to being ironic, as well as accepting the eccentricities of their peers as if they were the norm. Therefore declaring oneself to be bisexual was nothing that would cause dirty looks; on the contrary, people end up liking you even more. Even so, I took my time in telling Julia about Amanda, or about how I was attracted to our photography teacher. I had the feeling that she wouldn't have such a favorable opinion as the guys who spent all evening playing pool in the decrepit hall in the student union. The weeks flew by, and it became increasingly difficult to raise the subject.

Julia and I were parked in a small street on the south side, sitting in the car, passing a joint between our fingertips, when finally I told her. Julia exhaled smoke through a crack in the window, gave a little giggle and said: "It's not as if I didn't know, Cora."

It was a shame to turn up late to my own personal life.

That night, and the nights that followed, I was forced to overcome the shame of having kept an open secret. We went out together more and more. We never invited anyone else. Julia still didn't like beer, but she began to drink *batidas*, which involved low quality alcohol mixed copiously with condensed milk. One moment her gaze would lose itself in the dim waters of the Guaíba, the next she would focus on me. One day, she moved closer and gave me a kiss. Then that became more or less the norm: both of us drunk, in the back seat of the car, in motels that charged very little for two-hour stays, in dirty restrooms at gas stations.

Amanda met me one afternoon in a snack bar to say that I always seemed to be annoyed at her, so the best thing was for us to stop seeing each other. I didn't put up a fight, even though I felt strange watching her get up and leave. I stayed there, nibbling a straw, while there was still some juice in my glass. Then I got up and started walking down the busy street, completely oblivious to the hustle and bustle, the medical appointments, the ergonomic mattresses, the nightstands, the carbon paper, the nightdresses, the people with nowhere to sleep and the crack addicts, the rustic furniture store that was clearing stock. As was the case almost every other night, I had a date with Julia.

Two hours after leaving the Bertussi brothers' memorial, we arrived in São Francisco de Paula. There was a pretty lake, five minutes from the center, which Julia remembered having visited on a school trip. The Alpine-style mansion in the background had lingered in her memory too, although at that time she didn't know it was a hotel, the Hotel Cavalinho Branco.

If that building were a person, it could only have been a very dignified gentleman with a walking stick and some macabre ideas in his head. Naturally, we went inside for a look. The porter was on his coffee break, munching on a slice of bran cake. He wiped his mouth and greeted us. We asked for the rate per night. He told us the price. I looked at the acrylic prints of landscapes of Rio Grande do Sul and felt depressed. He said: "It's low season, I can give you a discount." Julia turned to me and twitched her shoulders, just a tiny spasm, as if she agreed with the idea of staying there as long as it was me who publicly stated our intention. "This building is historic, it was going to be a casino," the porter explained. "But then the president at that time, Eurico Gaspar Dutra, signed a decree prohibiting gambling in Brazil. It never even opened, it was still under construction. Imagine the job opportunities if they hadn't banned it. Dumb country, don't you think?"

As I filled in the form, I tried to imagine the last night of

Brazilian casinos. I saw that eleventh-hour spin of the roulette wheel in a hall full of mirrors in Copacabana Palace. Everything in black and white, of course. The crowd around the table, men with dark, slicked-back hair, women in long gowns with cigarette holders, doing their best to be seductive, with so much going on I nearly missed seeing the winning number (I was, apart from anything else, entirely inappropriately dressed). Fourteen, red. A man became discreetly elated, silently punching the air.

"Third floor, on the right," said the porter.

We went upstairs. The wallpaper along the dark corridors exuded a slight odor of mold.

We were in the room now. It was already nighttime. Julia had pulled a chair up to the edge of the bed and was sitting on it, slipping her size 36 feet, dark nail polish, tiny star on the back, under the long outdated bedspread (was chenille the name of that fabric?). She stared at me, as if to check that there would be no tricks. As for me, I was standing in the middle of the room. I stretched out my arm and grabbed one of our bottles of wine from the table. I had removed the seal a few minutes earlier. Then, I picked up one of my boots and lowered the bottle into it, so that it sat in the heel.

"You won't manage it," Julia said.

I gave her a confident smile. It was simple, I'd seen tutorials, even drunk people could do it. And what's more, I'd once seen it with my own eyes, Jean-Marc, by the banks of the Seine, against the stonework of the most famous bridge in the city. What was Jean-Marc doing now? I began to beat the Doc Martens against the wall. I must admit that my far-from-subtle trick to remove the cork made one hell of a noise. It seemed as though I was trying to bring the whole building down, bit by bit. Julia watched me incredulously, and even I was no longer quite so certain that it was possible to substitute a corkscrew with a mere shoe. But giving up was out of the question. When the stopper finally began to give way, and a tiny bit of cork peeked out above the mouth of the bottle, immediately transforming my clumsy maneuver into something of a miracle, our tension gave way to a fit of giggles. I laughed at how much Julia laughed, until I had no strength left in my arms. Luckily, the cork was already halfway out. I dismantled my contraption and put the bottle on the table. The dark liquid was shaken up, tiny bubbles surging to the surface.

Julia tried to compose herself. She breathed deeply, straightened her spine.

"Is that what they've been teaching you in Paris, Cora?"

I felt proud to be the girl who didn't need a corkscrew. I picked up two tumblers from the top of the mini-bar.

"I'd say so. Among other things."

"And here I was thinking the French were a bit more elegant."

"They know how to live."

The wine was terrible, but I didn't say anything. You just had to drink it to forget. On the whole Brazilian wines were truly awful, with a few exceptions that I certainly hadn't had the pleasure of trying.

"Nice wine, isn't it?"

"It's okay."

Julia lay on her front to adjust the iPod, legs dangling, swinging from time to time. The device was linked to two speakers. I turned the other way. There was a kind of balcony, not big enough for someone to sit on, but from which I could now see the lake and a few dim lights amid the patches of fog. I stood outside with my wine glass.

"Hey, you have this album."

An agitated, energetic guitar began to play. It was the start of "The Song Remains the Same," the first track on Led Zeppelin's best album.

"God, it's a long time since I've heard this."

And what if I said that I hadn't either, because it reminded me of those nights in the residence, and I wasn't sure whether returning to those nights was such a good thing. If it hadn't been for us, the record player would have been thrown out. Mathias was getting rid of old junk. Mathias was getting married. I wasn't invited. There would be a big celebration at Clube Comercial de Soledade. The only chance that someone like that lady with the bright lipstick, itching to get on the dance floor, would get to wear that imported shade of red, which slipped through the checkout almost unnoticed at the Rivera tax-free store, between the Black & Decker drill and her husband's three bottles of Ballantine's. Julia wasn't exactly enthusiastic about the wedding. She kept saying nasty things about the family and some of the other guests she'd have to encounter, which for me was a novelty. Where had this cattier version of Julia come from? Could I have had something to do with it?

Julia spoke less and less about her family. She no longer went to Soledade every weekend, although she still wasn't able to tell her parents that she stayed in Porto Alegre because she wanted to. On the phone she still had to resort to some kind of excuse involving her studies. We continued going for drives or listening to vinyl in the residence. One of the two of us had the idea of the Unplanned Journey. And yet neither of us lifted a finger to move. Driving around within the city limits. Playing music at low volume so as not to wake the sisters. Talking about the trip.

"And you could drive," Julia said one night, drunk, like I was, "and we could go really far away and then we'd get someplace, and the place would be pretty as anything, and there wouldn't be anyone there, and we could stay a few days, or weeks even, and then decide whether or not to come back."

More or less a month later, Julia announced, in an almost mechanical tone, that she was going to study in Montreal.

I was still on the balcony, looking towards the lake. It looked as though the fog that was hiding sections of the landscape was forming directly above the water, giving the impression of a really lousy special effect in a horror movie. It wasn't believable, even though it was happening. Only dregs of wine remained in Julia's glass.

"It's 'The Rain Song' next," I said.

She sat near me, half inside half outside, leaning on the doorframe.

"It's a nice one."

She swirled the wine round in her glass, as if it would reveal a secret message or some kind of prediction of the future. Down below, for a few seconds, car headlights lighted up the narrow gravel path leading to the parking lot. There was a moment of silence, then the banging of doors. I took a step towards the balustrade, in time to see the new guests pass under the arch at the entrance. A small and adorable family of three.

4.

THE CHINESE BOY was carrying the dragon as if it were a salver, pushing his way along the chaotic Rue du Faubourg du Temple. Sixty-odd teeth that had been perfectly shaped into spikes in the back of the patisserie, and yet were entirely devoid of any sense of nobility. The door of my building banged behind me and I greeted the lad, whom I often saw carrying the Styrofoam structures. He moved his head slowly and returned my greeting. When I started walking, he was already way ahead of me.

Paris was blue that day. Paris was blue every single day in January. The sun left the scene and was replaced by a kind of oscillating neon light that looked on the verge of breaking down. The green of the dragon, further and further away now, was the only green that would be seen until the leaves started to bud again in the trees, surrounded by more cigarette butts than soil. I lived right in front of the patisserie that provided the Chinese community with its Styrofoam sculptures, on the fourth story, view of the street, one single window. A hundred and sixty square feet in total. It smelled of fried food when they were frying, cigarettes when they smoked. Once a week, it reeked of Peking-style eggplant.

I had been in Paris for almost three years, and this wasn't my first address in the city, or the smallest. I had lived, in the following order, in a single bedroom rented from an old lady, in two university residences, a top bunk in a post-graduate's room, on an inflatable mattress set up in the living room of an employee of the Brazilian embassy. Let's just say that the apartment on Rue du Faubourg du Temple was the belated fulfillment of my initial fantasies of Paris. Not by chance, it had appeared at a moment when my life seemed to be relatively calm, although when it came down to it, I sometimes doubted that it was what I was really expecting from my days in France. So, every morning, I walked to the discreet door of a place called the Olivier Gerval Fashion & Design Institute, where I was no more than a regular first year student of fashion. Sitting in one of the middle rows, I never asked questions, no matter what the subject, the history of brocade, corsets, accounting, was Chanel a lesbian, who invented flares, why is a bias cut best here? Then I went home to make lunch.

In the afternoons, I slid sandwiches along a stainless steel counter near Notre-Dame until seven, repeating the names of the ingredients in English, French, or if necessary, a hesitant Spanish with a hint of an Argentinean accent. On that particular Wednesday in January, however, my daily tasks wouldn't be carried out quite up to par, so to speak. My dad had sent me an email on Sunday, and I hadn't felt able to formulate a response quite yet, not even something as simple as a yes or a no. I decided to leave the apartment as early as possible. Far away from the computer, my conscience would weigh less heavily.

Two blocks to the left, and there I was, in front of the café I often visited, although rarely at that time of day. The Christmas picture—a snowman with a fake smile hurling snowballs at two children—still hadn't been removed from the window. I pushed open the door. It was strange, but I had never seen more than four or five people in the place, and that morning there were even fewer, just two elderly men sitting at the counter, talking in low voices, contemplating their glasses, searching for crumbs. A Willie Nelson song was playing. When Jean-Marc came to serve me, I had already taken off my coat and all the accessories needed to survive a winter's day. "Fucking cold," I said, and he replied: "You seem to have learned to complain like a real French girl." I smiled, ordered a coffee and a croissant, and I watched Jean-Marc move away. He had a tattoo on his bicep with the name of a girl from long ago.

During almost three years in Paris, I had naturally met a lot of people. From Namibia, from the swamps of Louisiana, from the totalitarian remains of Estonia and Ukraine. Men of Arab descent served me overly sweet teas. Japanese girls described their Tokyo and Kyoto homes to me with the assistance of electronic translators. At my birthday party on the banks of the Seine, I was given a Peruvian hat and a bottle of tequila with a slightly smoky taste. As for my love life, it also followed a global logic. I *frequented*, as the French would say, an Algerian neighbor whose apartment constantly issued the interminable wails of *kabyle* music. And, at more or less the same time, I had met a nineteen-year-old Argentinian girl called Alejandra in an indie bar called Pop In. Jean-Marc, however, was the first French person who really wanted to talk to me.

The previous week, I had had lunch with Alejandra in a tiny Vietnamese restaurant where the dishes cost peanuts, and I was on my way home, alone. Walking at night. Perhaps that was why so many Brazilians left their country, switching graduate jobs for kitchens and masonry work, and never mind the tiny apartments they'd have to face, never mind family far away, never mind wages that barely stretched, we just wanted the simple pleasure of walking at night. That's what I was thinking about. I was almost home. The café was dark, the sign switched off and chairs on the tables. Jean-Marc was sweeping the floor. Behind the glass, his silhouette was light, dynamic, and occasionally he would take surprising little leaps, like a character in *West Side Story*. I found it amusing. I kept watching until Jean-Marc noticed I was there. He spun around holding the broom close to his body. As he came to a stop, he saw me. Then he walked perfectly normally towards the door, stuck his head out, with no visible sign of embarrassment, and said: "Can I offer you a Kir Royal?"

"Is it Cassis you put in that?" I asked, as soon as Jean-Marc set the glasses of red liquid down on the table. I had never tried a Kir Royal.

"Cassis and champagne."

Jean-Marc sat down in front of me. His hair fell to his shoulders, a few gray strands, fingernails of a guitarist. At precisely that moment, I remember having thought that Jean-Marc was happy in his job. It was good enough. He would never wake up thinking about why he was still a waiter, or blame his absent parents, the years of glue sniffing or the ascent of right-wing politicians. I took the first sip and said it was great, really. He smiled.

"You said you're from Brazil, right?"

"Uh-huh."

"Funny, you don't seem like your average Brazilian girl."

"What's your average Brazilian girl, the kind you meet in Bois de Boulogne?" He laughed. "What do you think I should do to make my nationality more obvious? That is my intention, after all."

Jean-Marc slipped his hands behind his head and stared at the ceiling, but the moment of reflection didn't get him very far; he soon opened his arms in a gesture of defeat.

"All I know is that Brazil has beautiful beaches, I'd really love to see those beaches. What do you call those wooden houses in the hills? Favelas, is that right? I know something about favelas too. Oh, and aren't you champions in plastic surgery?"

"Maybe."

"Yes, you are. I saw a documentary about it."

"Nowadays you can learn pretty much everything just by watching documentaries."

"Precisely," he said enthusiastically, missing the irony in my observation.

I started to go a little slower with my Kir Royal.

On the other side of the window, the street was almost empty. The streetlights imbued the dirty stone of the buildings with a warm yellow glow, corresponding with the common perception of the way the city should look. Despite the authorities' best efforts, however, there was a great deal of disappointment to be had. Cramped hotel rooms where romances came to an end. Bistros serving frozen food. The Mona Lisa was much smaller than anyone could imagine. The Greeks left the same old shards of crockery on the ground to attract tourists in Rue de la Huchette. Young Hemingway fans walked the banks of the Seine clutching blank Moleskines. Paris was the perfect setting for a story that wasn't actually happening.

I turned back to Jean-Marc. He was rolling a cigarette. He had placed a clump of tobacco on the paper, spreading it out more or less evenly, and was now rubbing his thumbs and index fingers together to close it.

"But what are you doing here, studying?"

"Yeah, I started a fashion course. In September."

He gave an incredulous laugh, then ran his tongue along the adhesive strip.

"Seriously? That'll kill you, girl."

"Too late."

"I mean, you've got style, that's for sure. But you don't learn to play Beethoven so you can start a rock band."

"I don't suppose so."

I gave a reserved smile. I wasn't particularly interested in debating the point. Jean-Marc asked whether I'd like another Kir Royal, I said yes, please. He stood up. I looked at the tattoo. I had never managed to see the whole thing, but I could make out some of the letters, perhaps an I and an E.

"What does it say?" I said.

"Sophie."

He raised the sleeve of his t-shirt.

"Ancient history."

"Looks like it was done yesterday."

"I got it retouched."

"Do you still love her?"

"No. God, no. But I have a deep respect for my past."

That was my conversation with Jean-Marc one night, after which I went for almost a week with entering or even walking past the café, until that morning. I took the last bites of my croissant and searched for my watch under the many layers

of clothing. I had less than fifteen minutes to get to the Olivier Gerval Fashion & Design Institute, where I would spend
the next few hours watching the evolution of the silhouette
throughout history, the only guy in the room (gay), and the
pigeons on the neighboring roof. I picked out a few coins in the
palm of my hand, then tossed them into the little tray. Jean-
Marc came out from behind the counter. When he reached
me, I was already on my feet, and the old men were laughing
at something a certain Bertrand had done. One of them began
to cough. Jean-Marc was standing in front of me, not picking
up the coins, as if he was concentrating on something I was
completely unaware of. "What is it?" I said, as I put my coat
on. He leaned his elbows on the back of an empty chair.

"You off to class?"

"Yes. Late like a Latin American."

Jean-Marc laughed.

"You're funny, Cora."

"No one's ever said that, as far as I can remember."

"I was thinking, can I have your number?"

"My number?"

"What would you think if I asked you on a date?"

Then I was gone. I had hurriedly pushed open the café door
and, once I was out on the street, set off in the opposite direction from my fashion degree. I, the girl who used to go to
Montmartre to buy fabric, who went all the way to a haber-
dashery on Rue des Archives to find yellow buttons the size
of a two-euro coin, had suddenly decided not to go to class.
The sky was overcast with cold. I had the feeling that all the
clouds might join together at any moment in a single heavy

mass of about forty square miles, in other words, the size of Paris, which, after all, is an unbelievably small city. I fastened my coat to the neck. I was walking towards the Saint-Martin canal, which extended from La Villette, in the northeast, to the public marina of Bastille. A pretty manmade watercourse, with locks and small iron bridges worth walking along at the weekend. I did that sometimes. The streets became pedestrian areas on Sundays. Little kids, new couples, old warriors with their initials carved on ebony canes, they all stopped to watch when a lock started to open, and I must say it was probably one of the slowest processes I've seen in my life.

A curious fact about the Saint-Martin canal: for about two thirds of a mile, it seemed to suddenly disappear. This was because it ran the length of Boulevard Richard Lenoir, between the lanes of cars coming and going, following an unseen subterranean path whose only contact with the surface was via a few air vents. This was exactly the route I took that morning, equivalent to the hidden part of the canal. Twice, I examined the big vents. Dark. Very dark indeed. I said a word out loud, it came back to me. Which word? I don't know. I searched in the flowerbeds for a stone, then threw it in and promptly heard the sound of water. Someone raised an eyebrow at me. So I started walking again.

The truth is that big problems become even more problematic during winter. Even memories can be somewhat compromised when your toes are frozen. At the age of sixteen, I watched my dad force two suitcases into the trunk of his Monza Classic. I think I was on the veranda, so I had a good view of that dissatisfied man filling the car with shirts, pants and socks that he hadn't even chosen, in front of a house that no longer belonged to him. This didn't seem to signal a particularly good outlook for me, but, when I put my egoism to one side, what I felt for my dad was admiration. What he was finally giving up wasn't specifically that wife, that house, that daily life with that daughter; he was courageously relinquishing a greater concept, that made even true love seem like something manufactured in China. Marriage. "Marriage is shit." That was my way of articulating it all at the age of sixteen. I saw the car pull away, and I returned to my room and cried.

Deep down, I couldn't have been more wrong in my belief that my dad just wasn't made for marriage and family, which to my eyes seemed like a great virtue. I saw my dad as a rebel, a fighter, someone who doesn't conform, no sir, and that protected me, for years and years, from a much greater fall. Then came his girlfriends. But that wasn't a problem, because they barely lasted. The very notion of a girlfriend intimated the transitory nature of all those women. The first. The second. The third. You get used to it. The fourth. Why memorize names? Pick one and add Roman numerals. The fifth. The sixth. Not bad for a man of forty-six. The seventh. Jeez, you were quick with that one. The eighth. The eighth. The eighth.

The eighth was called Jaqueline. Jaqueline taught English, my dad was among her pupils, and she was twenty-seven, two years older than me. That means we had watched the same cartoons before school, eaten the same kind of biscuits you can't get any more, we sang the same irritating jingle for a banana flavored gum, and we were shocked, albeit without really understanding, when Ayrton Senna didn't make a bend. I can't say I particularly liked having the same childhood memories as my dad's girlfriend. This did seem, however, to point to an imminent break up: one day, Jaqueline would surely realize that she needed someone who was more willing to party, with a bit more hair, and, more importantly, that if there was something unresolved in her relationship with her own father (there must have been), the best way to confront it certainly wasn't with a boyfriend twenty-five years older than her.

But I was wrong. Jaqueline stayed. Jaqueline spent Friday and Saturday nights at my dad's apartment. Jaqueline moved into the apartment. One day Jaqueline confided in me her desire to marry. A real party. I kept the secret, but she didn't. The celebration took place without further ado. I had always wanted to live in Paris. I wasn't enjoying my journalism classes at all and, what's more, Julia had gone away. So I moved to Paris.

And now my dad was having a child. I'd been digesting this news for months. Even so, perhaps because I was thousands of miles away, it still seemed rather unreal to me. My half-brother, however, was already a concrete element. I knew, for example, what his name would be (João Pedro). I had seen the ultrasound, as well as photos of his future bedroom (bespoke furniture that already included a desk for studying). Thinking about it, perhaps any lack of concreteness was actually in me. Of course, I received medical updates, photos of the belly, lists of boys' and girls' names, reports as the pregnancy progressed. But all of that only went to show exactly where my place was, on the outside.

While Jaqueline ran her hand over her basketball-sized stomach, turned over and went back to sleep, it was morning in Paris and I was arriving in the Bastille. No matter which boulevard you approached from, the first thing you saw were the hordes of cars whizzing round the imposing column, as if caught in an infinite state of reverence to the golden angel on top. It could be noisy, so much so that I felt the need to move on and leave behind those streets filled with the bicycle bells of attractive women on their way to encounters in quiet cafes, and all the metro entrances, and the stairs to the opera house, where young men with dramatic hairstyles would sit, fifteen-year-old girls smoking, skateboarders in tight pants, and a number of gay boys who had only just realized. All that was sufficiently far away now and once again, the waters of the Saint-Martin canal emerged.

I sat on a bench. The boats anchored in the marina gave the impression that they would never leave it. Not far from me, some men were playing *pétanque*. I watched the silver balls for a good while, trying to work out whether it was any different to the Brazilian version of the game. But the truth was that I didn't really know anything about bowling, except for the story of a third cousin who had his finger ripped off by a bowling ball when he was little. Luckily his parents were quick enough, and they put the finger in a bucket of ice cubes and dashed to the hospital. It all turned out fine. I stopped watching the *pétanque* players.

No, I don't think I wanted to be in Brazil in March, when João Pedro would arrive by caesarian, because all Brazilian women have caesarians now. I could certainly miss ten days, a fortnight of classes, as my dad suggested in his email, then again in three voicemails on my cell, perhaps I could take some work for the journey, but why would I do that? I was freezing, and a slight ache behind my right eye started to nag. I stood up. I was walking along an empty sidewalk when some people came into view. They were leaning on the low wall, looking towards the canal. From left to right: a bearded man smoking, a woman in gym wear, a man in an overcoat holding a suitcase.

"What is it?" I asked them.

"A boat's passing. They're opening the lock."

So I joined the group and waited.

When Jaqueline appeared in my father's life, it took me a while to realize that she was just what he was looking for, nothing more nothing less, young and foolish, basically, at precisely the time when I was very busy being young and foolish too. I was betting on any lame horse that appeared in front of me, rehashing the same old dramas until they wore out, I told myself that I had no expectations when expectations were my only fuel.

I would spend all day thinking about Julia. Then night would fall and I didn't want to have to accept that we had come to the end of the line. Our final incursions into the city seemed to be a poor imitation of those that had occurred just a short time earlier. I went to the same places to try to generate the same situations. That gas station. The bar where the Doors cover band used to play. We ordered two Brandy Alexanders to go, they tasted the way they always did, and the lid kept coming off the disposable cup if I drove too fast, but it was no longer funny. "Slow down," Julia might say. And that was a novelty for me. I didn't know where that freshness of the previous months had gone. From being secret lovers—although the role made me uncomfortable, I admit there was a certain charm in it—Julia and I had regressed to being best friends, who occasionally, very occasionally, took things a bit further.

Not that I had been consulted about it. Nor did I feel like starting a what's-happening-to-us style conversation. So Julia stayed with her boys, and I led my own life. I didn't like university parties. I would prefer the three subterranean stories of a gay club, where the music, even if it wasn't the kind I'd listen to in any other context, at least sent the entire dance floor into a state of pure excitement. Meanwhile, Julia was shaking her thing in a club hired by the Electrical Engineering students. Julia made it to the Faculty of Medicine's famous hundred-day party. Julia dressed as Penelope Pitstop for the Architecture Department's costume party. She told me the following day about the boys she'd been with, students of all kinds, they would be shy, or perfectly adapted to ordinary life, or bipolar megalomaniacs who were proud of their madness, some of them were convinced that they had only to study management to become millionaires, others operated on the back legs of dogs that had been run over at four in the morning, and there were others who spoke about skeletons of unfinished bridges in the middle of the jungle and the theme of childhood in the poetry of Manuel Bandeira. None of them, however, had won Julia's heart. That was the part I could call consolation.

But our story came to an end as a huge storm swept over Porto Alegre. That night, eighty-three trees were ripped from the ground by winds of over sixty miles an hour, telephone wires tangled round the branches that fell, everything went dark and people were forced to wonder for a moment whether they had any candles in the house, and why there were any candles in the house in the first place, while the thunder reverberated and the streets filled with water like a kiddie pool. I was with Julia in the Maria Imaculada residence. The sisters had no problem finding candles to burn, but they didn't want the young students playing with fire in the solitude of their rooms, so the third floor living room was packed with girls. Legs draped over the side of an armchair, Elisa lamented the fact that she was missing her eight o'clock *telenovela*; not wanting the evening to be a complete waste of time, she was filing her toenails in the semi-darkness. Four girls were playing cards around a flame that glowed in the center of the table, every round followed by an explosion of laughter, while others lay prostrate on sofas, pondering their fatal tedium. Julia turned to me and said: "Let's get out of here." We climbed the stairs with our arms stretched out in front, one step at a time.

Because the room was pitch black, I instinctively went straight to the window as soon as Julia opened the door. The headlights of the few cars venturing along the avenue allowed a glimpse of the sheet of brown water extending across the asphalt, and you could only guess where the edge of the sidewalk was. I witnessed a bus cause a small tidal wave, then I looked back into the room. Where had Julia gone?

"Julia?"

"Here."

From her voice, I could only assume she was sitting on the bed.

"I have to tell you something, Cora."

"Have you fallen in love with someone?" I said abruptly, gazing into the black void of the room. For an instant, Julia remained silent. As if my hypothesis had more foundation than I imagined.

"I'm going to Canada. In a month."

"But why don't you wait for the holidays? I don't think you'll take long to . . ."

"I've been accepted at a university in Montreal. I mean, to finish the course."

"Oh."

I was so shocked at the news that I hadn't even found it strange that Julia had been able to tell me with such sobriety and self-control.

"Are you happy for me? You should come and stay."

"You never told me you wanted to go to Canada."

"It isn't something I've been dreaming about since I was little. It's just something that happened."

"Something that happened? No one called you begging you to go, how can this be 'something that happened'?"

"I filled out some forms, all right? And I got in, it's that simple."

I could hear the rain falling on the zinc roof in heartrending shards.

In fifteen minutes' time, the lights would flicker twice and finally the power would be restored, raising cries and applause from the girls gathered on the third floor, and then I would slam the door of Julia's room, run down the stairs, colliding with some of them, smiling on the way back to the relative comfort of their rooms. I would reach the ground floor with the feeling that I had swallowed cement, and that this was the last time the sister at reception would bid me goodnight, out to Avenida João Pessoa, a deserted corridor, garbage bags swimming in the flow, part rain and part sewer, my socks sodden with the first step. The rain streaming down my cheeks wouldn't seem so terrible.

But there were still fifteen minutes to go before the power returned. Julia let her sneakers drop onto the parquet floor, one foot, then the other.

"When did you submit your application to the university?"

"I think it was a couple of months ago."

"A couple of months? Christ."

"I didn't know whether they'd accept me."

"So? Two months? How could you have done all this behind my back?"

"This isn't about us, Cora."

"Of course not. It's never about us. Never."

In January, when my shift at the sandwich franchise came to an end, the sky had been dark for at least two hours. I said see you tomorrow to Corrine, the other employee, then crossed the square in front of Notre-Dame. Few tourists were there at this time of year, compared to other seasons. The Gothic building shone. Somewhere on that complex, allegorical façade, there was a man holding his own head, but that meant nothing to me. My parents never forced me to take first communion. The fattest book on the shelf in my house was always *Don Quixote*.

Coming towards me, surely on the way to some bar in the Latin Quarter, was a group of teenagers, four guys, two girls, and all six were wearing I PARIS t-shirts under their open jackets. The wind blew more strongly, I shrank into myself. The tallest of the boys looked at me when we were close enough. Ah, those silly fedoras tourists buy! Do they ever wear them again after they go home? I hoped so. But perhaps that kind of courage, the kind you need to wear hats, was restricted to the wild days spent in cities that aren't your own. I turned the next corner, then walked down the stairs to the metro station. My train didn't take long to appear.

Once I was settled in the carriage, I put my rucksack on my lap and opened the pocket to get my cell. No calls. Alejandra had gone to Morocco. Jean-Marc would probably wait until Friday or Saturday to call. As for my dad, the first theory was that he was pissed at me; the second was that he had finally understood that he needed to respect my time. Either way, the time had come to reply to that email.

The blue canvas curtain was shut across the window of the Chinese patisserie. I keyed in the code and entered my building.

At that moment, I never could have imagined that after eating two slices of toast with goat cheese and firing up the computer, hoping to distract myself with the news, a window would suddenly pop up to obstruct the lengthy reports on the European crisis, and that that window would say Julia, and that that window would say: "Hi, how are things? It's been a while." She was often there, I mean, her name was, sometimes even a photograph, a snowy park, a cake straight out of the oven, the stage of some concert, that sort of thing. That was all I knew about Julia in Canada. So why had she chosen that particular night to tell me that she was now nearly qualified as a journalist, but not remotely satisfied with her job as a photography assistant for the website of the *Montreal Gazette*? Her parents had gone to live at the beach. She might take a vacation and stay there a whole month.

She wrote: "I'm going to link up the camera." I saw her new haircut and the empty room where she was sitting. Cardboard boxes were piled up behind her. Julia could see: my bed up against the wall, the mosaic of postcards and magazine cuttings above the headboard, my smoky eyes.

"Wanna see where I live?" she asked.

I said I did. Straight away, the computer was on the windowsill, pointing downward. I began to laugh. My insignificant voice telling her to be careful was lost to a Montreal corner. There was a pedestrian crossing. The light changed from red to green, the cars began to move between two rows of bare trees. It was snowing and the tires left streaks on the tarmac. Remember that trip? Remember that trip we never took? Two hours twenty-seven minutes later, I wrote the email.

Hi dad, how are you?

Sorry I didn't reply before. The course is tough. I'm busy working on the sketches for a collection to present at the end of the month. It's based on some aspects of gaucho clothing, like espadrilles, hat, *bombachas*, those embroidered waistbands, etc., which I plan to adapt into street-wear, with some elements of rock thrown into the mix. At least that's the idea anyway.

About me coming to Brazil, I agree. Thanks. I'm going to have to miss some classes, but that's fine, I can talk to the teachers. What else, is everything all right there?

Listen, I need to sleep now, it's late already, but we can talk properly during the week, about dates and other details, all right?

Miss you all.

Kisses

Cora

5.

JULIA AND I STAYED A SINGLE NIGHt at the Hotel Cavalinho Branco. On a morning that dawned fresh and bright, we bought the accessories needed to make a proper maté infusion, a bag of coarse ground *erva-mate*, a gourd with the traditional patterned band round the bottom and a plain silver straw, then we set off towards the canyons. It was a smooth drive, no one else wanted to be there, the kind of road we wanted desperately. On either side, the undulating fields were like hurriedly laid table cloths. There were tractors. Soya. Small wooden shacks. I was listening to some hilarious tales about one of Julia's childhood friends, as the wind whipped her hair into a terrible tangle. I stretched out my arms as we went round the bends, all ten fingers gripping the wheel—the countryside immediately shifting on its axis—and, finally, back on the straight, I turned to Julia. She was always in the middle of something.

"But the strangest thing about my dad is that he used to make matchstick models, have I told you that? First it was all sorts of bridges, then the Seven Wonders of the World. He exhibited them at the Clube Comercial, I was ten, the whole of Soledade was there. It was really embarrassing."

"I wonder how you survive something like that."

"Hey, it was traumatic, all right, big city girl? You wouldn't make it a week in a place like that."

The hand-painted name of a general store. Three wicker chairs placed expressly for the purpose of observing the passing cars. We stopped to buy fruit and water. The elderly proprietor asked: "What are two young ladies like you doing here?" The light slanted through the windows, drawing luminous streaks of dust that seemed to point at the pinkish potatoes in a basket, as if a direct message from the heavens. A quick shot of palm fruit *cachaça* for Julia, please, while I paid the bill. On the street, she bent down and said: "Look at the insects clinging to your car." I moved close. I could smell the clouds of alcohol. "There's blood here," she concluded, taking a small step back, then moving forward again, rather fascinated. We stood looking at the red spots that had spurted from mosquitos caught mid-air.

"We're carrying the blood of strangers," declared Julia. And then she laughed to herself as she got into the car.

There we were, on the road again. Pieces of orange and grapes dropped onto the rubber mats. I took bites of succulent plums, then tossed the remains from the window, like in the days when you believed that watermelons would grow from the black seeds you spat out in the garden. I still didn't know what to do about Julia. It was the fourth day of our trip. Until that moment, neither of us had made any mention of our previous parting of ways. If it had never been a big deal, why would it be now? Perhaps it was better this way. But it reminded me of Jean-Marc on Pont des Arts, opening that blasted wine bottle with his shoe, and all those padlocks signifying eternal love around us. Couples visiting Paris would write their names on padlocks and leave them on the iron bridges. Were all the keys at the bottom of the Seine? I had told Jean-Marc about Julia one sunny Sunday. I said: I was in love with a girl who just wanted to have fun. He replied that I shouldn't feel sorry for myself, that it can happen between a man and a woman too, which he could confirm from his own experience, laughing as he said this, his back against the railing, I was surprised the padlocks weren't hurting him. But when you like people of the same sex, I continued, the relationship can get really confus-ing, I mean, the signals, the signals are more obvious between a man and a woman, right? Like flirting with your best friend and making yourself understood? "This is the universal prob-lem, Cora," said Jean-Marc with a smile, as he took a rubber band from his pocket. Then he tied his hair in a ponytail.

"But what's the deal, asking me for advice?"

"I don't know, you, God, this is going to sound really strange. I think it's because of your tattoo. Not exactly because of that, but because of what you told me in the café, 'I have a deep respect for my past,' do you remember that? You seem to understand stuff. I'd say you've passed the test with this love shit."

"My God, then that's the only test I've ever passed."

Jean-Marc fell silent. His eyes began to follow the move-ment of the passersby. On the Seine, a *bateau-mouche* crammed with people was approaching and, when it got close to us, those on board waved to those on the bridge, who returned the gesture with equal enthusiasm. For as long as there had been boats in the world, waving had been irresistible.

"Did you fuck this girl?"

"Of course. At my house. In public restrooms. In a load of motels."

"Motels, eh?"

"The Brazilian kind, you'd find them *exotic*."

"Go on."

"You arrive there in your car, okay, in the middle of the city, you ask for a room without getting out, you go in, park in a garage, like the garage of a house, see, and in that garage there's a door that leads you and your girl, or you and your guy, directly to the room. The room usually has a mirror on the ceiling, a round bed, that kind of thing, as well as clean sheets in plastic bags and cheap champagne in the refrigerator. You stay there for two or three hours and pay something like fifteen euros on your way out."

"And you're telling me she was the one who wanted to have fun."

"It wasn't like that, Jean-Marc. At the time I didn't have much of a choice, I lived with my mom. I would show up at home with Julia the odd Saturday and say: "Mom, Julia's going to stay over." But I couldn't always do that."

"Got it."

"But it doesn't matter now. I'm going traveling with her in March, in the south of Brazil. We haven't spoken for almost four years."

"Sounds fantastic. Beaches?"

"No, no beaches. I'm scared."

"Of beaches?"

"Of Julia. Of myself."

"Have you ever put a chocolate mousse in the freezer?"

"I've eaten a chocolate mousse that's been in the freezer, if that helps."

"Right, so the part that's exposed to the air gets hard, but it's still delicious inside, yeah? It'll be the same with this Julia, don't worry. You just need to get through the first layer to find everything that was there before."

"Strange analogy."

He stared at me. I frowned.

"Chocolate mousse? Delicious inside? Honestly, Jean-Marc, I expected more of you."

Jean-Marc burst out laughing. He stood up. Then he held out his hand for me to get up too.

"Did you think it was chauvinistic?"

"Terribly chauvinistic."

We took our wine and went for a walk round the Jardin des Tuileries.

The day was filling up with clouds. Julia wasn't speaking much any more. She had reclined her seat and picked some jazz with a stormy expression. Chet Baker singing. As we passed the final road sign for Cambará do Sul, all that remained was a narrow band of clear sky above the horizon. The town appeared right after the abandoned carcass of a cream-colored Chevette.

A good ten years ago, Cambará do Sul was increasing in popularity. Aerial views of the Fortaleza and Itaimbezinho canyons appeared in miniseries on the Globo channel; a couple kissed in a frost-covered field in the final scene of a commercial for a certain cell phone operator, so that people like my mom's friends began to take an interest in the idea of "a bit of a rest" in "such a beautiful place." Along the edges of narrow unpaved roads, on land that was practically worthless, guesthouse sprang up, with restaurants offering French service.

There were lakes. Ducks. Hydro-massage baths with a view. Gas heating in log cabins. Sheepskins draped over armchairs. The cold seemed to be part of the fun, if not the best thing about it, after all the town had extremely low average temperatures, coming second only to the little-visited and not-too-distant São José dos Ausentes.

The guesthouses frequented by my mother's friends, however, about which I had heard many times, were nothing more than a handful of delusional islands in a visibly poor district. The end didn't seem far away. I looked out of the window and everything seemed sad. It would be difficult to find a picture of Cambará do Sul to put in a tourist pamphlet. What about parabolic antennae stuck in patchy lawns? What about houses as thin as paper with too-narrow windows? What about the stray puppies rooting in the gutters? Even so, those things said very little in respect of my own first impression of the place. Perhaps I should concentrate on the main street. I was sure that Julia was doing the same as I was as we rolled along it, that is, drawing comparisons with the towns we had already passed through, coming to the obvious conclusion that there was something inhospitable and rather oppressive in the air. While in other towns girls went out arm-in-arm to eat crepes or check out the discount rail in a clothes store, in Cambará do Sul the residents moved as if numb, tired of themselves, heads downcast, and alone. Almost all of them were male. Men who walk like that are men without jobs, I thought. Men standing on corners are men without jobs. Men playing pool at three in the afternoon are men without jobs. Men sitting in squares in front of closed churches are desolate men without jobs.

"We should stay in that hotel," Julia said suddenly, tapping her finger on the glass. I pulled over to the curb and leaned over her for a better look.

"*That* hotel?"

It was a wide building, right up against the sidewalk, with a row of green windows on the second floor. A bar occupied part of the ground floor. A hoard of unemployed men was there too, under sheets of corrugated iron, smoking avidly, as if the cigarettes had been offered by the jailer the night before the execution.

"Why not?"

Those mischievous eyes of hers lighted up. Julia had a peculiar way about her, always did: it seemed like she was thinking about sex even when she wasn't.

"Let me park up properly first," I replied.

That day, when we left the hotel for the second time, and the darkening clouds were making rain seem even more imminent, my self-confidence was pulsing sky high. I had put aside my anxiety to resolve everything quickly. We walked down very quiet streets where there wasn't even always a sidewalk. Light was also quite scarce, which led me to think that either people must go to bed very early, or were doing their utmost to economize.

I was wearing the red leather jacket, the wide hood balancing over my head. I had the impression that simply having put the hood up made me more dangerous or at least less vulnerable, which couldn't be said of my traveling companion; her imitation leather leggings went perfectly with the t-shirt dress on top, cardigan with tiny buttons and the perfect little jacket, but the ensemble made her seem like some poor girl looking for a party that wasn't even close to starting.

We were a couple of strangers wandering around when we met Beto and Petal. It all began in a street running parallel to the main thoroughfare, in front of a well-lighted courtyard. There was a Ford Rural parked between the iron gate and the garage door. I didn't know much about cars, as I've already mentioned, but of course I could identify an old-style two-tone Ford Rural in the middle of a sea of popular silver cars. With the trunk facing the street, half cream, half green, the roof like something of an afterthought, the jeep looked like it could have left the factory floor and traveled in a vehicle transporter that same week.

"I wasn't expecting that," said Julia.

"Pretty cool."

"It's more than cool. I'd swap your car for it."

"Very funny."

"You think I'm joking?"

When the jeep door swung open, I was starting to think about moving on. But by then it was too late. A girl's legs dangled for an instant. She was wearing a calf-length skirt, which ballooned up to cast a shadow in the breeze when she jumped to the ground. Tiny drawings in ballpoint pen covered the fabric and rubber sole of her sneakers. Waves, hearts, a bird. I looked at the girl's face, and she seemed to have been smiling for centuries. I pulled down my hood.

"Sorry," Julia said before anyone else could speak, "we were just admiring your car."

"That's fine." She kept standing there, with the same expression.

"I mean, is it yours?"

"Yeah, yeah. Mine and Beto's," replied the girl, as if Beto was an old childhood acquaintance of ours. She had a pretty face, but the kind that you look at now and feel sure that it won't look so good in ten or fifteen years. In time, her jaw would give her the appearance of an inverted triangle, especially if she kept the long straight hair. And that Germanic tendency to flush in the cold weather would, in the not-too-distant future, cover her skin with fine, dry lines.

The car door was still wide open. Seeming to remember this, the hippie girl turned briskly and disappeared inside once again. Only her feet remained on the outside. When she returned, she had a bag slung over her shoulder, the kind you use to help save the environment. She stared at me. She seemed to be waiting for my contribution to the conversation.

"We're not from round here," I said.

"I know."

There was a silver stud in her nose.

"Did you arrive today?"

"Yes, this afternoon."

"Then you haven't had a chance to get out of town and see the canyons."

"No, not yet."

"It's really worth doing. The rest is shit."

Julia and I started laughing, then exchanged a brief glance.

"I'm Petal," the girl said, approaching the low wall. "Yes, my parents were creative. But once I met a girl called Sap, and then it didn't seem so terrible."

"Petal isn't bad," I replied, lying unashamedly.

Then, Julia introduced herself and, leaning across the wall, the two women kissed each other on the cheek. I would be next. Before placing her lips against my face, Petal asked what color my hair was, she liked it so much, but I didn't want to say that I dyed my hair in France, because that would sound conceited, so I just replied that I couldn't remember what that particular shade was called. She smiled when I said my name. She put her arm around my shoulders and kissed my cheek, just once, as is the norm now in the south of Brazil, or among people of a certain age group, at any rate. Then, someone inside the house shouted her name, and she yelled back with all her lungpower, slightly annoyed, which was a surprising new side to her, "Coming!" Turning back to us, she adopted her former sweet expression.

"You girls aren't vegetarian, are you?"

"Not likely," Julia replied.

"Excellent. Because Beto's making *carreteiro de charque*, and if there's something he really knows how to do right, it's salt beef."

It was chaos inside. As if a group of children had invaded the house, jumped on the sofas, surfed the rugs, pulled the books from the shelves and then piled them precariously on a coffee table in the center. "Sorry about the mess," said Petal, and replaced a pillow that had fallen on the floor, a gesture she could have made ten hours earlier. "We had some friends round yesterday." The ashtray overflowing with stubs suggested that it had been a long night.

When I told the story, many months later, of our encounter with Beto and Petal, the first thing I would mention was that our night seemed to be endless too. I wondered how predictable it had been, after all, that we should have shown up when we did. How many times a week did the couple entertain strangers? Who were the people who had been there the previous day? I never found out. But I had rarely met a couple as friendly as Beto and Petal. The two demonstrated an unusual interest in what others had to say, or at least in what Julia and I had to say, which probably stemmed from the belief that all humankind is good, and that no person is worth more than any other. Even though neither Julia nor I had much to contribute when it came to subjects like adventure tourism, park conservation, community orchards and the old-fashioned mindset of people from their hometown of Caxias do Sul, Beto and Petal talked at length, enthusiastically and knowledgeably, about all those things and, eventually, asked us: "But what do you think?" They weren't just being polite; it seemed more like a kind of radical leftist tic. I had nothing against it, anyway.

At the start of the night, the four of us stood in the kitchen, Beto at the stove. His dreads were held back by a dark blue rolled up bandana, and the black tank top he wore must have already been through the wash about four hundred times. Petal topped up our wine glasses whenever they were half empty. I told them about opening bottles with shoes and they couldn't stop laughing. They'd lived in Cambará do Sul for a year and a half, providing tourism-related services: they demonstrated how to extract honey, they offered transfers to Parque Serra Geral and Parque Aparados da Serra, pointing out native plants and describing their benefits, they organized excursions to waterfalls that were often known as *the wedding veil*, they promised wild places you'd never manage to get to alone, and they gathered broom from the roadside to prepare teas to be sampled with colonial products from the region. The rest of the time they enjoyed life, as everyone does when they've just entered the realm of their twenties, but let's just say that these two had an extra dash of spirituality.

So I was drunk, and things were beginning to get a little more complicated. Petal was chopping parsley, her back to Julia and me. I heard the noise of the knife snapping the thin stems, as I watched the pleats of her skirt fall from her hip, sometimes swaying almost in slow motion, to one side, then the other, finally returning to a vertical position. I thought about sudden curves under cotton panties. I thought about skirts slightly shorter at the back. I thought about Catholic schoolgirls from some country that wasn't ours. And finally, I thought about Julia undressing in the hotel room, in a kind of optimistic anticipation of later that night.

I didn't have the slightest idea what was being said. When I came to my senses, my eyes were fixed on an empty Formica counter. I looked for the others. Petal was tossing the chopped parsley into the pan. Julia was looking in my direction. Beto had disappeared.

"Where's the bathroom?"

It was down a narrow corridor. I suddenly bumped into something. Someone shouted: "Cora, are you okay?" and I replied that I was, but I stood there for a while in the dark, my back against the creaking wood. There was a spider somewhere. I remember the fear more than the spider. Then I went through the nearest door, which turned out to be a bedroom. The rumpled covers in the middle of the bed looked like they had been picked up off the floor and dumped there, the mound illuminated by a beam of light from the street, a car passing slowly, perhaps looking for an address, which granted me an opportunity to witness Beto and Petal's admiration for the East. I had seen those elephants somewhere before, with their rear end facing the door, good luck, that was what they meant, I think; other people's beliefs always seem more interesting than our own, but Turkish nazars aren't any better than a handful of rue, and the millennium-old coitus practiced by Indian figurines can't beat the natural breasts of a Russian prostitute.

They were all sitting round the table when I reappeared. Beto served me an enormous plate of his salt beef and rice stew. I held my hand over my glass to prevent Petal from refilling it. I began to eat, I praised the food, I was starting to feel a bit better. A draft came in through the cracks in the house. Julia was looking at me, Petal looked at me occasionally, but never the two of them at the same time.

"I have to tell you something." Beto crossed his cutlery on the plate. "You have to go to a town called Minas do Camaquã."

"Nearby?" I asked.

"Quite far away. In the pampa."

Petal smiled.

"Tell them about the playboy who owned the place."

"Baby Pignatari. He dated Brigitte Bardot."

"Brigitte Bardot went to the pampa?" Julia asked, astonished.

"I don't think so. But Richard Gere got it on with a girl from Bagé."

Julia and I burst out laughing.

"Hey, I'm not kidding," said Beto. "It really happened."

Shortly after Richard Gere came up in conversation, Julia's cell began to ring. She pulled it out of her jacket pocket, and why it was in her jacket pocket was something I'd like to know. How long had Julia been waiting for that call? She said hello a few times, the signal seemed terrible, she decided to go out to the street. The door slammed. Petal stood up to serve me more wine, and I let her fill my glass above the level of good manners.

"But what's in this Minas do Camaquã?"

"Nothing. That's the point. It had copper. Now it has nothing."

When Julia returned, we sat on the sofa. I eyed the tower of books balancing on the coffee table for a while. There was the complete works of Carlos Castañeda, some Neruda poetry, Latin American novels, biology manuals, history books that mainly covered the military dictatorship in Brazil, all of them precariously piled on that table, as if at the end of the previous night someone had tried to locate a certain passage, unsure as to whether it was part of a sonnet or some journalistic report. I opened a book at random. *The Teachings of Don Juan.* A dedication dominated the first page, in a large, curving hand, red, so firm that it had marked the following two pages. *Beto, for an incredible week, with all the love in the world, Luciane.* I shut the book and put it back on the pile. Castañeda was pure lies.

On the way back to the hotel, I remember that I kept searching for the moon with the insistence of someone who's had a few too many. The porter was napping, but he recomposed himself as soon as we entered reception. He turned to the panel and took key number eight. Ours was a sad room, with that single sixty-watt bulb hanging from a wire. Julia went into the bathroom to get changed.

As I watched the strip of light escaping through the slightly open door, I told myself that it didn't look like a good sign, or that at the very least it was a reversal of my expectations from the start of the night. Thinking about it, perhaps it did mean something positive, as the naturalness of undressing in front of friends can only be explained by your lack of desire for them. I had never been naked in front of my classmates at high school. If I was ever forced to, I'm sure I at least turned my back, which might have seemed ridiculous at the time, but which years later became one of those immediately obvious clues in the psychologist's office.

I fell asleep before Julia emerged from the bathroom.

Not a single drop of rain fell in those wee small hours. The wind had carried the clouds far away and, the following morning, an uninterrupted sun shone over Cambará do Sul. We were standing in front of the hotel waiting for the Ford Rural to arrive. The brightness was troubling me.

"Drink a bit of water." Julia held out an aluminum bottle on which was written *fabriquée au Canada*.

"Ta."

"Don't you have sunglasses?"

"Left them in Porto Alegre. What an idiot."

"Cora."

I squinted and turned to face her.

"Eric called me last night."

"Ah."

"Don't you want to know what he said?"

"I guess so."

"He said *Hey, Julia, tell me where you are, exactly, I'm coming to see you.* And Eric, you know, he's never been interested in Brazil."

"I don't think it's a question of him being interested in Brazil, Julia."

"I know, but—when things were good between us, I really wanted him to come with me."

"And now?"

She thought about it.

"Not now."

We remained silent for a while. Around us, we could hear snatches of conversation, as if the living dead of the previous day had some reason to feel better now. A woman walked past, talking loudly into her cell phone. Another had bought a dozen warm bread rolls, the plastic bag sweaty between her chubby arms. I took a few steps forwards and sat on the sidewalk. Beto and Petal were at least ten minutes late.

Julia followed and stood next to me. I raised my head and shielded my eyes with my hand.

"But I could never imagine Eric here, see, doing this trip," she said. She seemed to regret what she had said before.

"That's fine," I replied, and looked ahead again.

"What is your problem, Cora? Why are you so quiet?"

"Just call him and say you don't want him to come."

"Calm down, I told him that yesterday."

"You really said that?"

"God, of course I did! I don't know why you need to be so mistrusting of everything, I mean, why would I lie about this? I told him I was going to keep traveling with you. That I didn't want him to come at all."

Now it was she who was getting angry. I tried to smile, but I feared that it was too late. Then, relieved, I said: "They're here." And I stood up. Julia turned round to look. Inside the jeep, Petal was waving frenetically, as if it was still necessary to call our attention to the fact that they had arrived. We waved in return, with slightly less enthusiasm. The Ford Rural was even more beautiful in the sunlight. Beto pulled over to the curb. It was Julia who moved first to open the door. Turning to me, she retorted: "Anyway, I've turned off my cell."

That really got to me and I climbed into the back seat without much in the way of niceties. For the start of the journey, I spoke only when necessary, smiled only when necessary too, thinking, as I looked out of the window, about that last utterance of Julia's. It seemed like the vindictive conclusion of a conjugal row. The couple is arguing and suddenly the wife says: "And look what I bought for you today," tossing the now meaningless surprise of good intentions into the other's lap.

The journey to the canyons wasn't as tough as I had imagined. Occasionally the car had to zigzag in order to avoid the ruts in the track. Just imagine a man throwing an entire sack of gravel into a deep hole. That was the noise the road made. All around us was an infinite countryside, with a few horses, always alone, like the lost pieces of a plastic toy farm. If you watched for a while, you'd be surprised at their sudden bolts down the slope, which weren't to escape from another animal, or to get to water or food, nor to find other horses, but, so you would think, just for their red manes to stand on end, for their hooves to barely touch the soil, before they came back up again; those horses ran like the wind, not to put out a fire or mend a broken heart, but just because they wanted to have fun. I felt rather jealous of those horses.

Inside the car, the climate was improving. Julia had now spoken to me directly, sometimes her eyes even demanded contact with mine. Whether this was because we were in the company of other people and therefore had to keep up appearances, I couldn't say.

"Look at that over there. Now *that's* a hotel."

Beto pointed to the left.

"They have towel heaters in every bathroom, you know? Towel heaters," he added, as if that item was the height of superfluity.

I leaned over for a better look. The immense grounds were surrounded by a high wall. From our position, however, it was possible to survey the entire hotel as it had been built on top of a hill. It looked like a drug baron's house, but with some aesthetic consideration. I kept imagining my mother's friends draping over loungers, drinking cocktails that tasted of their youth.

When we caught sight of the archway at the entrance to Parque da Serra Geral, Beto reduced his speed to almost zero and turned round. Not for a car that might have been coming, nor for a detail on the roadside that he'd forgotten to show us; Beto looked directly at me and at Julia.

"Do you have any idea how beautiful the two of you are?" I think he had been observing us in the rearview mirror for some time. "Seriously. Apart from Petal, of course, I've never seen girls so sexy and stylish."

Well, the canyons were truly impressive, with plateaus and crevices, like they'd been swallowed by the earth and were fighting to stay. Everything was green, looking like moss from a distance, but it could have been grasses, bushes, trees, reminding us how it all began with the breaking up of the supercontinent Gondwana, and here the four of us were today, walking under the sun. We had seen the sea. There was a piece of land at the bottom, divided into plantations, then came the coast, a strip that was just slightly bluer than the sky. We sat at the edge of a precipice to eat our sandwiches. The stone was warm. I thought about my little brother who would be born in a week. I thought about Eric, and whether Julia might have used me to make him jealous, whether he would have come to Brazil if she had said yes, whether she really had said no.

We passed ten or so people in a circle, arms around one another's shoulders, in preparation for a long trek. One by one, they were telling the rest of the group their name, age and profession. Introductions made, the guide asked, in a voice that was accustomed to the unfavorable acoustics of the vastness, whether they had all remembered to bring sunscreen. One man had forgotten. The woman wearing a yellow tank top and a visor offered him her tube of factor thirty, and he timidly thanked her. He began to smear the cream over his neck, then his face, then his arms, with an expression of disgust. Apart from that group, there weren't many other visitors in Parque da Serra Geral.

The same couldn't be said for Aparados da Serra, our afternoon destination, where the famous Itaimbezinho canyon was located. Coaches were accumulating in the parking lot. This second park was less wild than the first. You could spend hours here without your skin reacting to any spiny plants. There were clean restrooms, picnic tables, a scale model of the canyons, school groups being restrained by young teachers with their hair in buns. We followed a paved trail. Julia and Petal had dropped behind at the first viewpoint.

Beto was walking briskly.

"Can I ask you something, or will you get annoyed?" he said, without lessening the rhythm of the walk.

"Shoot."

A couple approached from the opposite direction. I exchanged a polite smile when they passed.

"You and Julia, you're lovers, aren't you?"

I laughed.

"Why did you wait for that couple to pass to ask me that?"

"Who knows. I think maybe it was so I didn't embarrass you." Then he pulled the face of someone who isn't sure they've given the right answer.

"Do you really think that would embarrass me?"

"Well, to be honest, quite the opposite. I think it would be sensational if you are actually lovers."

"In the sense of 'wow, two girls together, how delicious' or in the sense of 'love is plural and infinite, it doesn't choose gender, race or creed'?"

Beto stopped.

"What are you talking about?"

"Forget it."

He stood facing me for a few moments. I could bet that Beto was the type to trust his own judgment. He had read the Carlos Castañeda books. He believed in energy configuration, luminous eggs, that kind of thing.

"I think I get it," he said eventually.

"Get what?"

"It's complicated, isn't it?"

"Not for me."

"But for her."

"Maybe, Beto."

Luckily, Petal and Julia had almost caught up with us. Julia said: "Tell Cora the story about the delegate." Petal told me about the delegate. Julia found it hilarious all over again. We continued along the trail, far beyond where the paving ended. Two hours later, we listened to an explanation about the area's geology in front of a scale model of the canyons and, rather unwillingly, looked round an exhibition of photography of regional birds. By that time, I was tired of nature.

The last thing we did together that day was to take a photo in front of Beto and Petal's house, with the Ford Rural in the background. Julia set the timer on the camera. We moved closer together and froze in a leer while the little light flashed on the device. Afterwards, we checked the image and concluded that we had all come out well enough.

When we left, after hugs all round, turned the corner and walked up the road in silence, I still had the feeling that we would see each other again. Perhaps somewhere else. There was a small piece of paper folded in my purse, and on that paper was the name of a man, the name of a stone, the name of a ghost hamlet in the poor pampa. It didn't rain. Julia and I ate soup in a basement diner. The table was near the fire. Thanks to a half bottle of *cachaça*, visible behind the counter, the hotel receptionist was fast asleep. I stretched out my arm and took key number eight. He opened his eyes when we began to giggle, and his head moved slowly to the left, but in seconds his eyelids dropped and he was asleep again, as if we were no more than part of a dream, as if it made no sense for us to be there.

6.

I HAD GLIMPSED A DARK STAIN right in the middle of the asphalt, but I didn't say a word. It wasn't far from the cars in smithereens and the ambulance with its back doors open. The light revolved over the scene like a mute family member. I kept wondering whether they bothered to clean the dark stains afterwards and, if they did, who would be nominated stain remover, would they be thinking about someone in particular as they doused the road with water, and would they have been informed of the owner of the pool of blood when there was no longer a pool there? Since we had passed the accident, I had thought about my mother several times.

Julia was now playing with the seeds from a slice of tomato. The earthenware bowl of bean stew had formed a viscous surface, which gave the impression of a mangrove swamp. I swatted away a fly, then another one. We were in a large dining room with fluorescent strip lights. Apart from our table, only two others were occupied: one, at the back, with four uniformed men and the other, near the door, with a woman and child. I crossed my cutlery on my plate, although it had been a while since I finished eating. On the television, a Palmeiras player committed the worst miss of the round.

"I'm going to call my mom, okay?" I announced to Julia.

She raised her eyes and nodded her head. I went out to the street, passing on the other side of the diner's large windows. For a moment, as I moved away, I watched Julia and the table and all the reflections as if they were all part of an Edward Hopper canvas.

The public telephone was set slightly away from the rest of the facilities at the gas station. I dialed the number and started looking down the straight line of the almost empty street. How long had it been since I had heard the voice for collect calls? Then that long beep.

"Cora, is that you?"

"Hi, mom."

"Why didn't you take my cell phone, honey? Where are you?"

She seemed breathless, as if she had hurried to answer the phone.

"I think it's a place called *Pan*tano Grande."

"Pant*ano* Grande?"

"Is that how you say it?"

"What are you doing in Pant*ano* Grande?"

"It's a long story, mom."

"Cora, listen. There's nothing there, honey."

"In Pant*ano* Grande? It's fine, we just stopped for lunch."

"It's not safe, none of this is safe. Is the main purpose of this trip to leave us here thinking the worst twenty-four hours a day?"

"Oh my God, no, mom. Why do parents always think that everything their children do is specifically to piss them off?"

"I don't know. But your dad has every right to be pissed at you."

It had been a while since my mother had ceased to measure her words. You could say it had been ever since the separation. When my father left our house all sense of subtlety seemed to abandon her, and so my adolescence was bombarded with the sincerity of a pessimist. It was as if I needed to have someone analyzing the world around me all the time and issuing regular bulletins about its (mal-)functioning. Beneath the surface, the message always seemed to be the same: you don't have to see with your own eyes, *I*'m telling you how it is. And so my mom would accompany me to the garage or to the front door with her last minute recommendations, the themes of which varied from urban violence to the bad influence of certain friends. Come on, I knew perfectly well how extreme it was to live in a big Brazilian city. A guy had fired a gun in front of my college. He didn't show up in a radio class because he was busy shooting on the other side of the street, and hundreds of students in dozens of classrooms were able to recognize the sound. Now tell me what a tragedy it is for a nation that its entire youth knows what a goddam firearm sounds like.

And of course I would make friends that weren't worth two cents, the friendly face just waiting for me to turn my back to then comment on my ripped jeans halfway down my ass, that little touch of exhibitionism. I would swallow all ten pills from a pack and throw up in the house of some guy whose name I didn't remember, and all just to grasp at some lousy rays of light. I would spend the entire night waiting for something that wouldn't happen even if I went a week without sleeping. I would fall in love with people who changed their minds too quickly. The wrongs just formed part of the rights, and I wasn't about to cry for the choices I had made, because, however hard the falls, I was left with the feeling that even they had their beauty. But my mom was always more afraid of life than devoted to it.

"I know he's right," I said.

A truck prepared to enter the gas station. Its brakes were issuing an increasingly shrill squeal. I covered my ears and had the impression that the driver was finding the scene funny.

"What? I can't hear you at all!"

"I said that your dad was really angry!"

There was a pause. In that time, the truck moved away, going to park behind the gas pumps, where two men in riding boots were chatting and sharing a single cigarette. I tried to see Julia behind the window of the diner, but the reflection of the sky left everything blue and shining.

"I think he'd like to know why he paid for a plane ticket for you when you're not here with the family waiting for his son to be born. Cora, listen to me. Two girls alone on the road, that's not a good idea."

"Is she still having a caesarian? On the 24th?"

"Oh, I don't know, Cora. Why don't you call your dad?"

"Maybe I will."

"This isn't France, understand? It's no good to be driving around down there, people don't do that. Was this trip Julia's idea?"

"No, mom."

"It's convenient when she doesn't have a car."

"I said it wasn't her suggestion."

"Sorry, hon, but I honestly just can't believe that."

I hung up as soon as I could, promising my mother that I'd call again in a few days. When I returned to the diner, Julia was no longer there. No one was there, not even the girl serving tables. Our plates had been cleared. The freshly baked cakes made the window perspire. I walked out again. There was a street vendor on the terrace, he must have been there a long time, although I hadn't noticed him before. I wondered why someone would buy a plush heart with the words *I love you* while traveling down the RS-290. When I moved closer, I began to hear something about violence in the Mexican cartels. Someone had been beheaded, just to make the message clear. Among the caps, fans and sunglasses made in China, a mini television was now showing the exterior of a single-story house surrounded by reddish soil, where the head had been found. The vendor was staring at the screen, sitting in one of those camping stools. There was a girl of about eighteen near him, probably a daughter, but she was filing her nails with her back to her father and the TV, wearing too much eye shadow, a foundation that made her orange face appear separate from the rest of her body, and a top revealing a couple of inches of flaccid belly. The man said: "Take a look at the sunglasses, miss?" I said no and entered the restroom.

The only light was the natural daylight from outside, which entered dimly through a strip of slanting windows. Four cubicles. I began to examine the gap between the floor and the doors. In the third, Julia's sneakers appeared. We had never swapped shoes, I don't think, although it was a regular practice among friends of a certain age and with a certain level of intimacy. Julia turned round, her heels suddenly swiveling into view. She flushed the toilet.

"Did you talk to your mom?"

"Mmhm."

She looked for soap, but there was none, in liquid or bar form. Resigned, she cupped her hands under the stream of water, which dripped into a chipped basin the color of dead skin. She looked for a paper towel, there were none. So she started shaking her hands, and with them shook the Navajo bracelet, the other times with Eric, the shared bed, the fits of homesickness, a road in the wilderness of Arizona. Some droplets hit my face. I closed my eyes and opened them again. The situation made me slightly nervous because it smacked of something that had already happened, me, Julia and a public restroom, there was a real labyrinth of public conveniences in my head, perhaps more than motel rooms, sometimes I had to ask for the key from the gas station attendant, sometimes it dangled from an empty carton of motor oil so that people didn't accidentally make off with it in their pocket. The walk to the restroom was always rather ridiculous. Julia would allow herself to be led. Then it was hard to say whether it was me pressing her up against the door, or her positioning herself, delicately, between me and the outside world.

Now Julia was inspecting herself in a tarnished rectangular mirror. A cloud had made everything slightly darker. I began to say:

"I was thinking that you . . ."

She drew close to me, just two seconds of certainty, she reached up to my mouth and, almost crazily, kissed me. When she withdrew, she was smiling, perhaps because of my astonishment. She bit her lower lip very discreetly in the middle of that smile.

"What were you thinking?"

I dangled the car key from my fingers.

"That you could drive for a bit."

Another smiled formed. She grabbed the key.

"I thought you'd never ask."

The road to the pampa was green and blue, and vast. Fewer people, more ruins. Nightclubs that had closed down long ago. Towns three digits away, indigenous men selling wicker baskets, a used car lot where tiny flags fluttered for potential customers that weren't there. Julia drove with the seat closer to the steering wheel than I did, which probably said less about our difference in height (a couple of inches of advantage for me) than about certain personality traits. In the rearview mirror, I watched things get small and then even smaller. Like the names of a couple of lovers written on a single grain of rice.

What was that goddam kiss all about?

At times, something like a shack at the side of the highway fashioned out of garbage sacks inspired us to launch into meaningful conversation; whether it was enough that we were sympathetic, and how much the barefoot indigenous kids knew about having been screwed over. At other moments, we played old songs and sang along, No Doubt, Silverchair, Alanis Morissette before her trip to India. That spiritual journey had killed rock, and all the rebel girls from 1996, who grew their hair long so they could shake it in the solitude of their bedrooms, grasped desperately to the last distorted guitars of an era. The baggy t-shirts would soon be switched for the awful 'baby' look. I remember it well.

"I must confess that I heard Jewel and liked her."

"For God's sake, Julia!"

Her arms were more relaxed on the steering wheel now.

"Listen, it was kind of because of a neighbor of mine, he gave me the Jewel album as a Secret Santa on my English course. Like a message. It said: 'You Were Meant for Me,' that's my favorite."

"That was everyone's favorite."

"Whatever, it was a clear message!"

"Okay, it was."

"He liked me too."

"I believe you."

"Do you have Jewel on your iPod?"

I began to laugh.

"Of course not."

It was after four when we finally arrived at Pedra do Segredo. From Cambará, we had spent a total of six hours on asphalt and a bit more on a dirt track. We were now in the center of Rio Grande do Sul, gateway to the pampa, something unprecedented for both Julia and me. Our families had never suggested a trip to Uruguay, which would necessarily have introduced us to the southern half of the state. Uruguay had duty free stores at the border, a melancholic capital and above all beaches, beaches with freezing seas, of which the most famous was without doubt Punta del Este. Many of Porto Alegre's more contemptible residents went to Punta in the summer. Until a few years ago, their cars would return covered in bumper stickers; the colorful emblems of Uruguayan casinos and hotels were one of those silly status symbols, as were the small dice from a certain brewery and the logo of a horse riding competition.

Julia parked my car in front of a small brick house where we were supposed to meet a man called Lauro. It was the middle of nowhere. We got out. Everything was so quiet that saying something in a loud voice would seem like a heinous environmental crime. We took a moment to stretch our legs. Suspended above what was perhaps the start of a trail was a wooden, hand-carved plaque that read: PEDRA DO SEG-REDO CONSERVATION UNIT. This path went on to disappear in the tangle of undergrowth after an abrupt bend. Even further away, at a distance that was hard to pinpoint, sat the secret stone itself, recalling the head of a furious monkey. In a cartoon this would definitely be the mountain where the exhausted hero would arrive after a thousand adventures and the stone would open into a magical passage to reveal a world that was full of advantages over the real world, beautiful women, muscular men, walls studded with diamonds, cooperation, peace.

The door of the brick house creaked.

"Afternoon," someone said.

I looked. There was a man standing there. He took a step outside, as if to allow himself to be examined. He was one of those bald guys who prefer to shave their head than to seem in any way incomplete, around forty, skin quite sunburned. The print on his t-shirt was of a beach in California, where he had probably never been.

"Hi," I replied. "You must be Lauro."

Of course it was Lauro. Beto had told us he lived here alone, in the rural belt around the town of Caçapava do Sul, taking care of those protected acres day and night. Before that, Lauro had lived for two and a half years in Pantanal, where he had led treks for eco-tourists, been bitten on the fingers by baby caiman, as well as being dumped by the love of his life, a very short Nicaraguan lady who was only in love with Brazil. Julia approached him and made the introductions. For a moment, I wondered whether it wasn't dangerous for the two of us to be alone with a stranger; shouting wouldn't help in this place, there was no one to hear us. Ah, but what idiocy, I thought immediately, apparently I'm acting just like my mother, because of that telephone conversation earlier, and the confirmation that my dad was furious with me certainly didn't help much either, even though it was impossible for him not to be furious under the circumstances and, well, even if he turned to cheap psychologies in search of an explanation, for example that I was jealous of Jaqueline and the baby, that I felt I'd been replaced, rejected, abandoned, he would no doubt conclude that accepting a plane ticket only to disappear into the interior of Rio Grande do Sul was what you might call rather a disloyal attitude.

"Rent it for about a week," Julia was saying when I started paying attention again. Lauro was leaning against the door-frame.

"The house at the mines?" he asked.

"That's right."

"Of course, let's go see it. It sleeps four. There are two double beds."

He took a discreet look towards the car.

"It's just the two of us," I said.

"Ah, good. Don't you want to come in?"

I said okay.

Inside, the place seemed even smaller, a single room, most of which was taken up by a brightly colored motorcycle. There was, as well as the motorbike, a closet with double doors, a single bed, a corner to make food, and a table with a computer. I stared at the screen in sleep mode. Family of sea lions. Aerial view with pine trees. Large block of blue ice.

"Huh, it's been a long time since I've seen Beto. Is he still in Cambará?"

"Mmhm."

"And you two came from there in one go?"

"Yes," I replied.

"Courageous, eh."

Lauro turned his back to us and filled three glasses with water from the faucet.

"I was born in Minas do Camaquã."

"Really?"

"Seventy-one, I was raised there, my dad was a miner, but it's a ghost town now. I mean, there are still some people living there, a few. If that's what you're looking for . . ."

"Precisely that," I said promptly.

He sat down at the computer. Julia and I stayed standing, politely sipping our water. What was Lauro going to show us? Photos of the house? I didn't need to see it, I just wanted to get away with the key and some directions, as long as it had a bed (and it did, two of them), it was all good. The map of Brazil appeared on the screen, in satellite mode. Lauro typed in a geographic coordinate. It took a moment for the country to disappear, eventually replaced by smudges that gradually sharpened. There was Minas do Camaquã. It seemed like a miniature town made by scale model fanatics. Everything fitted into one glance. The soccer field. The rows of houses. "In my day, it even had a movie theater, Cine Rodeio, you'll see the building," said Lauro. Then he pointed to a blue smudge, which looked like a lake but which wasn't actually a lake but a deactivated open mine that had been accumulating rainwater since 1996. The blur that had caught my eye, however, was a different one, further to the right, sand colored, four or five times bigger than what you might class as the urban perimeter. I asked what it was. Lauro replied, askance: "That's the reject." I didn't have the slightest idea what that meant, so I asked again. I had the impression I was touching on a secret. Everything that came out of the mines that wasn't copper, he explained, was thrown onto that piece of ground. Piles and piles of stone ground down for a hundred and fifty years. Ninety-eight percent of what comes out of a mine is useless, so do the math, nothing is ever going to grow there. A manmade desert. I think Lauro's father had been one of those men. Perhaps that was why he was here now, watching over a bit of native wood. Sometimes children must inherit the sins of their parents.

7.

"I THINK THIS IS THE PLACE YOU WERE TALKING ABOUT," I said.
Julia rearranged herself to get comfortable on the low wall, and
as her hips found a new position, for an instant, I felt her entire
weight against my thighs. Her knees pointed at the overcast
sky.

"What place I talked about?"

We could see the entire town from here. Barely a thing was
moving. Cockerels sang who knows why or where. The mine
wagons on display in front of Cine Rodeio seemed to be pining
for the depths of the world. Behind us stood the aged structure
of a billboard. What could it have been trying to sell people
forty years earlier?

"Okay, not exactly *this* place, but like an out-of-the-way
place, a place that's pretty much no place at all, get it? I can't
believe you don't remember that conversation!"

Julia turned to face me, her hair spilling across my lap.
Suddenly, she gave a little laugh that wasn't a yes or a no. I
smiled, resigned.

"I just thought it might be here."

We sat in silence for a while. We were in a strange part of
town; as well as the billboard, there was, on top of the hill, a

metal star stuck to a plinth about fifteen feet tall, as well as a tower that was freely inspired by the architecture of medieval castles. A spiral staircase, speckled with rusty holes, circled the exterior.

"Where did we talk about this place thing?"

"In the car. Then in the residence."

"Was I drunk?"

"Totally."

"Wild times," she said, drawing out the syllables.

Wild times indeed. Julia naked in front of me under a bluish light. Her eyes straining to pick out some horrendous detail in the decor, then standing up and walking as if her legs were glued together, trying to hide something that was honestly a waste of time trying to hide, while I said something along the lines of—what was I saying? I was saying: can I have a drink? Everything okay? I never thought you . . ."

I came back to Minas do Camaquã.

A friend once told me that the ideal length for pendants and necklaces should be determined by what you choose as a "point of interest" (yours to others), and not by any factors such as seasonal trends or your height, so naturally the smart girls chose to nestle their good luck charms, rare bird feathers, stopped clocks and silver turtles in that incomparably delicious region between the breasts. Julia appeared to be following this advice to the letter. And the fact that there was a saint dangling from it, well, I think don't think that made a whole lot of difference.

I kept watching Julia, Julia watched the town, the town watched the eucalyptus trees, and the eucalyptus trees might well have been striving to catch a glimpse of their home, the distant shores of Oceania. Then I said: "Shall we go back?"

"Sure."

It was our first day in Minas do Camaquã, if we took into account that the night before we had arrived too late and too tired to do anything other than find the house, eat and sleep. Contrary to my expectations, the town wasn't completely deserted, even less falling to pieces, although the number of people was clearly far lower than the number of properties, which led me to conclude that their owners must live elsewhere, visiting only when they had the time, when they got such a notion for isolation into their heads that they just had to fill the car with stuff and get there as quickly as possible. Julia and I had been told by an elderly man that all those houses used to belong to the Brazilian Copper Company, which had then organized an auction and sold them for peanuts a few years earlier, almost certainly with the aim of preventing the town from disappearing completely. When I say peanuts, I mean the price you'd pay for an old motorbike.

It was rather an odd town, to be honest, where cattle grazed the stubborn grass growing in the middle of the road. No cars, no people to be seen. A few scrawny horses roamed loose, up and down, as if they didn't need any assistance finding their way home. And what could be said about the Wild West-style movie theater? We were passing it now.

"When are you heading back to Paris?"

My face immediately revealed my shock. It must have seemed a disproportionate reaction, given that the question, to Julia, was banal enough. I couldn't put off that conversation any longer.

"I think we need to talk about that."

"Talk about what?"

"About Paris. My dad. My brother."

"You're an only child, Cora."

"Till Monday."

She stopped in the middle of the street.

"My dad's going to have a son."

"What? What do you mean, why didn't you tell me?"

"It's a long story."

"Did your dad get married again?"

"More or less. I mean, yes. I ran out of the wedding."

"And you didn't have time to tell me?"

"Didn't have the courage, I think. The thing is . . . I pulled a pretty shameful trick."

"You ran out of the wedding."

"No. Yes, that too, but . . ."

And so I told her about the plane ticket my dad had bought. Of course he was expecting me to be with him, with Jaqueline and João Pedro and my single mother, for all those weeks, but honestly the thing I had been most concerned about from the outset was sending my car to the mechanic. I was sure it wouldn't start after so long, and as soon as you arrived, Julia, I packed my bags and dashed off to get you in that crummy hotel near the coach station, where that guy knocked on the window to comment on my boots. If you must know, that seemed like a bad start to me. It's not like I'm superstitious or believe that things happen out of anything other than, I don't know, coincidence, but, damn it, sometimes I do see a message where there is no message. I should have stayed in Porto Alegre, everyone was counting on me at that moment, even though all along I had never intended to stay. Even before I said yes, dad,

I'll be at the birth of my half-brother, that prospect was actually a path that led me back, not to them, but to our trip. I've known that since we had that conversation. You showed me a corner in Montreal, I saw the boxes behind you, it seemed like there was something really wrong in your life, in that scene, basically, because of those boxes, I think it's times like these when people tend to take a step back, and I thought okay, I'm going to jump in and fuck the rest of it.

Julia was silent for a while. A man walked by and said good morning. A cream car passed, the color revealing a great deal about its age. Two long-tailed birds were looking for an eleçtricity cable. Then Julia began walking.

"Hey. Where are we going?"

"Home."

"What home?"

"The house we rented, Cora," she said with a smile, as if it was absurd that I might have imagined another meaning to that phrase.

It wasn't pretty. It was what you might call "just a house," the grass had grown long around it and, inside, the furniture appeared to be cast-offs from other places, with little defects that justified wanting to get rid of it, the sofa leg secured by a piece of wood, a counter with permanent hot pan marks, the television with only the bottom half of the screen working. The tables empty of knickknacks. The walls devoid of pictures. The closest thing to an ornament was the fridge magnet from the gas supplier.

I sat on the sofa. Julia was still standing, but there was a feeling in the air that something was about to happen. This must be what it was like waiting for the announcement of war in an African president's office, stepping up to the most power-ful telescope in the world, the spotlights flashing on stage while the star of the show is behind the scenes dressing in white and sequins. Julia sat beside me, her left thigh fitting into my right thigh, her left shoulder fitting into my right shoulder, as if we were Siamese twins before the separation. Then I slid on top of her. In a matter of seconds, she made herself comfortable underneath me, her calves resting on one arm of the sofa, her head on the other, a narrow two-seat sofa that one day some-one didn't want any more. Her kiss had always been so precise, so cerebral, why not, full of suspense, about-turns, withdraw-als, advances, that even when her whole body was engaged, Julia was still concentrating on playing cat and mouse within those narrow confines, pulling at my lip with her teeth, mov-ing away at the high point, then coming in again, re-forging the lost path, sweeping every corner of my mouth with her tongue over again. I lifted her t-shirt until I found the start of her breasts. The first curve was escaping slightly from the black lace trim. I found this carelessness exceptionally beautiful. I moved away for a better look, trying to prevent her from notic-ing my desire for contemplation. Perhaps *that* was too invasive. My next step would be to open the complicated little hooks on her bra. Julia raised her head and leaned forward to facilitate my efforts. Thankfully the clasp gave way before it became one of the frequent comical moments that uncooperative clothing provides. Julia then placed her hands on my hips for the first time.

"Can we go to the bedroom?"

Her voice had changed to another register, the B-side of a delirious record. I took her hand and didn't look back.

Although the blinds were closed, there was a little bit of light, which I didn't seem to have noticed even a short while ago, in the living room. It must have been the sight of the bed that made me think of it. We had never had sex anywhere well lighted, with the exception of restrooms at gas stations, and even then, as soon as we went out of the door, there Julia and I were again, in the middle of the night. The night is permissive like a distant uncle. It only has to end for all the flexibility of rules and the potential shortcuts to end too. The paths are longer in the daytime. All of which means to say that we had never screwed before sunset. Never in natural light, always in a half-light drawn by a lamp in another room, or under the dim glow of the static from a television screen. Afternoons, sharp. Nighttime, a blur.

In some strange and twisted turn of events, we were now kneeling on the bed. I had only my panties left on, Julia, nothing at all. I felt her body pushing me back and I gave way only a little bit each time, she came, I withdrew, and all those little withdrawals were, in all honesty, my way of asking her to please lay me down and stretch out on top of me, with her hair tickling my face and everything else. She laid me down. Someone began speaking in the neighboring garden. It was the hoarse voice of a longtime smoker, talking, talking, talking to someone else, who, in turn, limited themselves to agreeing at regular intervals. I smelled cigarette smoke, but beyond that nothing changed inside the room. Julia slipped her hand inside my panties. Her fingers slid like a pair of shoes on a newly waxed floor. Then I raised my hips and the panties disappeared. We listened to Julia finger the smoothest, sweetest song in the universe.

Something that can generally be said about girls who don't have much experience with other girls is that they tend to make the mistake of being too delicate. Believe it or not, they are afraid of hurting you, even though it's an unfounded fear because, well, I've had things a lot bigger than an index finger inside me before, you know? Julia had started out like all those naïve girls, really slowly, very affectionate, assuming that, because you don't like men in that way, all supposedly masculine characteristics, such as aggressiveness (which is sometimes confused with pure and simple initiative), should be immediately banned from the act of sex.

Meanwhile, I was trying my best to make things less pleasurable for myself. The club swimming pool on the hottest, most humid day of the year. I'm alone and I slip into the cool water. I almost lose a ring. I concentrate on that, I need to ignore the world if I'm to have anything to offer her, I hold my breath so that I lose hers, my tongue is saying it's good, nothing was ever this good between us and it could all come undone in a matter of minutes. She closes her eyes, I know, I take the occasional peek, then she digs her nails into my back without meaning to because women never quite know the length of their nails and the involuntary pain they can cause. Her voice no longer comes out in a whisper. The people outside have either fled or they're listening to Julia moan and then say my name once, as a period, Cora. She says it like that to remember while she forgets that once upon a time she was embarrassed, and that it was all nothing more than a terrible idea.

I was getting dressed now, standing next to the bed. Julia was watching me.

"Do you think that being attracted to a body that's the same as our own is slightly narcissistic?"

"What I think is that your breasts are bigger than mine."

"Very funny."

My jeans had ended up some distance away. I went to retrieve them. A coin fell from my pocket, and oddly enough, it was a ten euro cent coin.

"Wasn't it Freud who said that, about narcissism and same sex relationships?" I asked.

"No idea. Have you read any Freud?"

"Nah."

"But you'd go with yourself."

"Is that a question?"

"I think you would."

"Would you?"

"Not with myself."

It was Saturday, two days until the birth of João Pedro. As soon as Julia and I had put our clothes back on, we went out again. The hoarse neighbor was sitting on a deck chair in the middle of the yard. He wasn't cutting the grass either. His feet disappeared amid clumps of weeds. When we passed the fence, he woke from his torpor, starting to follow us with his eyes, until he finally asked: "Have you seen Baby's house?"

Baby Pignatari's house. We went there that afternoon. We jumped the low wall. There was an empty swimming pool and we sat at the edge of it, imagining the people who might have been there before, until it became a kind of game, the pieces of which were Baby himself, his friend with the beard, the woman in a yellow swimsuit, the housekeeper, an intricate plot of jealousy, pride and greed, in which the yellow-costumed woman played a crucial role. To such an extent that the pool wouldn't have existed, that waterfall, starting at the top of the slope and descending in stages, wouldn't exist, that fireplace in the middle of the living room wouldn't exist, and Baby wouldn't have thought it worth hiding out in the depths of Rio Grande do Sul, if it weren't for his devastating and uncontrollable passion for the woman in the yellow swimsuit.

We spied through windowpanes and tried to open doors.

The day ended without us realizing.

Standing in the middle of the street at eleven at night, we began to search for the most obvious constellations in the sky, but I soon realized that I was quite bad at it; not only did I fail to spot any of them myself, I also had enormous difficulty understanding precisely where Julia was pointing. Following a finger to a star isn't the easiest thing in the world.

On Sunday, we discovered some abandoned buildings near the river. The loose zinc tiles creaked in the wind, the ground was an explosion of dead leaves and bits of wood. There was a flight of stairs, the first couple of which had disappeared. In a doorless cubicle, at the back of the lean-to, a washbasin, and toilet were still intact in their place. Julia took black and white photos. Then, we carried on towards the small beach. The path suddenly became narrow, between the water and stone that seemed to have been hewn by knife. There wasn't a soul to be seen, which gave a rather apocalyptic feel to the landscape. A bridge appeared up ahead. It was like a fragment of a nonsensical dream that you hurry to take in when you wake. I walked closer to the river, my sneakers began to sink, Julia told me to be careful, I grabbed her hand despite not being particularly concerned, I mean, about the fact that I was losing my balance, then she took my other hand too, giggling, pulling me to a lighter section of sand as if I was completely incapable of doing it without her assistance. As for me, I allowed myself to be led. The slightest bit of physical contact is a victory in certain relationships.

One day until the birth of João Pedro.

After spending a while on the little beach, we returned to the derelict industrial estate. As soon as my car came into view in front of those slightly devastated, slightly dusty buildings that told the tale of deaths and begrudging changes, I had the clear feeling that it fitted perfectly into the scene. That made me shudder, but I said nothing. Julia took some more photos, hardly ever of the two of us. We got into the car and I drove off. A minute later, however, I stopped again at her request because, to our left, there were two long constructions like dormitories, and the mere fact that they were well cared for was noteworthy enough, but there was also a logo painted on the wall which took them to another level of strangeness. It said: PORTAL PROJECT. And, between the two words, an elliptical shape that any Freudian would call a vagina.

"It's all shut up," Julia shouted, after walking round the outside and finishing her inspection at the front of the building.

"The other one too."

We didn't find out what on earth the Portal Project was for a couple of days. We spent a long time having sex again and again. Julia said terrible things about Eric. We discussed the ending of *Thelma & Louise*.

Monday. I woke up feeling only slightly worse than an organ trafficker. My dad had never exactly been bad to me. Could I blame him now for his fear of growing old? If I were in my dad's shoes and suddenly a woman twenty years younger flirted with me, would I respond with a resounding no in the name of sexual equality? Or because poor middle-aged divorcées didn't stand the same chance? In case someone pointed a finger at me and called me envious instead of feminist?

I tried to talk about it the next morning, but, while I was chattering fifteen to the dozen, Julia followed my sudden verbosity with a little smile that to me seemed rather mocking, making no comment, as if she hoped that at any moment I would say that I was kidding, that I wasn't that bothered by it, that, to be honest, the only reason for me to have started speaking about my dad was to prevent us having to talk about the two of us.

Once again, the neighbor was sitting with his feet sunken in the weeds and his head lolling to one side of the deckchair.

We drove back towards the twin buildings of the Portal Project, the vagina portal. This time, a man was on his way out. We watched him. He dropped the key, picked it up from the ground, and only then did he turn in our direction. He had caught a bit too much sun in the last two or three days. He was wearing a short-sleeved shirt, his pockets stuffed full, and he didn't seem exactly exultant to see two pretty girls. No more than thirty. Gay, perhaps. He was called Lucian. Not Luciano, but Lucian, from Iporá, interior of Goiás. And Lucian had seen flying saucers all over Brazil.

So that was what the Portal Project was all about, the observation of flashing colored lights and telepathic conversations with beings from other planets. To tell the truth, I don't know why it hadn't occurred to me sooner. Lucian talked for a while, Julia humored him and, as for me, I hoped with all my being that we would laugh about all this later.

Several times a year, the group of ufologists traveled to Minas do Camaquã because, according to Lucian, it was frequently visited by extraterrestrials; there was a *relatively intense flow of craft* in the early hours of the morning, naturally, over the area devastated by the "reject." I didn't ask why the little green men had chosen such a place as their destination, even though my instinct was to rip to shreds those idiotic beliefs held by Lucian and the other followers of the Portal Project. As Lauro had explained to us a few days earlier, in Caçapava do Sul, the reject was nothing more than a desert of hundreds of acres, made by men, his own father among them, no need for other-worldly explanations, it was all entirely plausible, you go chucking bits of stone on the ground and pretty soon it's bye bye ecosystem. Regardless, all I could think while we were talking to Lucian was that someone needed to notify the ETs that they would learn a lot more about mankind, if that was indeed their intention, in the dirty, violent streets of a metropolis than in discreet visits to the middle of Kansas or the depths of South America. That just seemed to be a sign of stupidity. But my irrefutable argument was this: if they had developed their advanced technology to the point of traveling through galaxies and more galaxies to finally arrive here, why the hell would they lack the capability to create something as fundamental as fashion? My God, those same tunics every time!

The guys at the Portal Project were building a city in Mato Grosso do Sul. I'm not kidding. That's what Lucian said, that the guys at the Portal Project were building a city in Mato Grosso do Sul called Zigurats City, where all the roofs would be rounded or pyramid shaped, so that they would be ready for the events of the next six thousand years. What were the events of the next six thousand years? I haven't the slightest idea. But Lucian had to get going. Bye, Lucian. Say hi to those nice folks from the eleventh dimension.

Monday 24th March, the day João Pedro would be born. We turned on Julia's cell. No signal. Then Julia went home, saying "good luck." She gave me a kiss. I went off to look for a public telephone.

Collect call. A fortune-teller's visiting card was stuck to the machine. It was windy, a fresh wind that bent all the treetops in the same direction; I turned to the side and for the first time noticed a restaurant that was simply called restaurant, the sunlight falling in such a way that it was impossible to make out anything other than the door.

Bring back your love, said the fortune-teller.

My dad didn't answer the phone.

It wasn't until the fifth day in Minas do Camaquã that Julia decided to talk about her little brother. It had all begun one afternoon with a stupid fight with a classmate called Marcela, who at the age of twelve had already built a solid and definitive reputation as a bad girl. Marcela would run to see the boys skin their knees on the coarse sand of the playing field, Marcela used the tips of her sneakers to flip over dead birds, bats, and cats (dried blood stains on the rubber soles of her Reeboks), Marcela would ask barefoot vagrants, practically mute, with booze breath and scabs from the advanced stages of illnesses, where they lived, how their families were, whether they had a photo of a loved one in their pocket.

She had dark eyes like two total eclipses, very fine eyebrows, the kind of childish nose that would struggle to hold a pair of glasses, at that moment perhaps she didn't have the slightest suspicion that she'd become a very pretty teenager, and that her dad would die in a head-on collision on the RS-386, on the way back from a group dynamic for the vacant position of warehouse supervisor.

When Marcela was nervous, she repeated Bhaskara's formula under her breath: x equals minus b plus or minus the square root of b squared minus four a c over 2 a. She must have read the formula in one of her sisters' exercise books, because the sixth grade were still learning multiplication and division of fractions with Miss Suzana. Marcela was the youngest child. Her family and Julia's lived on the same hill, just six houses apart, which led naturally to an intimacy forged less out of mutual friendship than inertia and the tedium of never-ending summer afternoons. To get to Marcela's by bike, there was no need to even pedal. Julia would drag her Caloi Ceci out of the garage, place some toy or board game in the basket because her friend had no more than three Barbies, hand-me-down building blocks, a Care Bear and a box of peg solitaire, and so Julia would cycle down the street, legs dangling, hands firmly gripping the handlebars, for yet another stifling day at the bad girl's house.

That afternoon, however, Julia arrived with her basket empty, frothing with rage. She pedaled in spite of the downward slope. Her dad had recently spent a few days in São Paulo and had brought her back one of those plastic replicas of a pool of vomit. The vomit had been an instant success at school. It was placed in classrooms and restrooms and the library and on the long counter in the science laboratories. A girl *nearly* vomited before she realized it wasn't real. The laughter was shriller than ever. Julia was proud. But a fortnight had passed, the fun had moved on, the vomit lay forgotten in a closet full of old toys.

And then her mother whispering, that day, after lunch:

"Ju, get that thing your father brought you. I want to show it to Aunt Marcia."

Marcia smiling and helping herself to maté.

When Julia opened the drawer, the vomit wasn't there.

Then she remembered she had called to ask Marcela over to play the previous Thursday. She recalled that Marcela had been pulling strangely at her t-shirt the entire time. She recalled Marcela suddenly remembering that she had to help her sisters with some new layout of the living room.

She answered the door herself.

"Can I come in?"

Julia doesn't wait for an answer.

"I'm just finishing off my geography homework. But we can go up, if you want. Have you already done yours?"

"Your living room's just the same."

"Living room? Oh, yeah. The thing is, my mom and dad didn't like it. And they were right. No one had a clear view of the TV."

Julia climbs the stairs in front. Marcela comes right behind.

"X equals minus b plus or minus the square root . . ."

"What are you saying?"

"What do you mean?"

"What's that you're whispering?"

They enter the bedroom. The geography exercise book is lying open on the desk.

"Nothing. I'm not whispering anything."

"Square root of b squared minus fou . . ."

"Again!"

"What did you get for number six? I know nothing about hydrography."

"Where's my vomit, Marcela?"

"Vomit. That plastic one, I don't know, have you lost it?"

Julia heads for the wardrobe. She knows that in the second drawer up Marcela keeps the three Barbies, the hand-me-down building blocks, the Care Bear and the box of peg solitaire. At the age of twelve, no one would come up with a better idea than putting a stolen toy in with the others. As soon as she understands what is happening in her own room, Marcela stands behind Julia and tries to tug her back by the shoulders, not at all gently.

"Stop that, I didn't take your vomit!" she shouts.

There's no one else home. Julia strains in the opposite direction and manages to stay where she is, but, when she bends down to reach the drawer, her knees waver and she falls on her behind on the floor. That just makes her more annoyed. She gets up again, while Marcela manages to conquer a tiny space between Julia and the wardrobe, and the fight starts to get really ugly, Marcela tries to stop Julia's hands, Julia escapes and retorts with small punches to the legs, pinches on the arms, Marcela says in a malevolent tone, "You should be looking for your little brother instead," to which Julia doesn't pay the slightest bit of attention, because her fingers are now on the drawer handle, and she pulls, and the drawer opens and, on top of the box of building blocks, is her vomit.

Then Marcela sits on the bed as if she weighs two hundred pounds. A very intense light explodes through the blinds behind her. Some of the light spills between the slats and falls in broad strips on the nightstand, where two objects occupy the side closest to the bed, a Bugs Bunny clock (present from Julia, his arms are the hands of the clock) and a diary with a padlock. Julia has never seen this diary before. She'll think about that later. She looks back at Marcela. At that moment, it's hard to say whether Marcela feels humiliated or sorry, or both, her bare feet dangling just above the floor, tears starting to cut a path down the middle of her cheeks, everything exasperatingly silent apart from the occasional snuffles and the tick tock of the Bugs Bunny clock.

"Why did you tell me to look for Mathias?"

She sniffs harder.

"Not Mathias, stupid."

"What are you talking about?"

"Your dead brother."

"I've only got one brother."

"Everyone knows about it, except you."

It's two o' clock in Soledade. Dona Neiva is at her window on the other side of the street, as always, watching for action that never happens. A slight smell of gasoline wafts over from Peixoto Garage. Julia freezes for an instant. Even if Dona Neiva has always been at her window, even if the fuel vapors have hung over that block since before Julia was born, those two pieces of information will gel together today with the typical precision of unexpected facts. She collects her bicycle and starts to pedal. After a few blocks, the houses become sparser, the yards fuller of junk, the walls give way to stumps and barbed wire. She's always been afraid of passing alone, but now it doesn't matter. A pig squeals. Julia can now make out the roof of the old mill, ten minutes out of town, where two streams of muddy water meet. All small places like to have something big to show off, and that, apart from grinding wheat, has been the function of the building for decades and decades. She has never been inside. That's something for older kids. She sees bicycles in the shade of the trees, she drops hers there too.

The mill is like an L on its side. On the long part, there are a number of names in spray paint by people with serious handwriting issues. *Big Head. Spud & Ana Maria 4ever.* But the world of vegetation is battling for space with the graffiti tags, some of which have already been covered by the highly adaptable leaves and branches. Ferns grow ten feet high out of the concrete. A creeper has begun to infiltrate through the holes left by the empty windows. If Julia were to stand in front of the mill for about ten years, she would see nature take the upper hand, part of the building collapse, rain enter through the battered roof, a green carpet of moss cover the gaps in the planks, the insect colonies, the birds, the rodents driving their teeth into an old noticeboard, but she's in a hurry now, she skirts the building, finds an opening between two damp planks, and then she crawls inside.

The ceiling is quite high, perhaps magnified by the fact that she is now in a gigantic space with nothing more than the diagonal slats of wood above her. She hears laughter, she can't tell whether it's Mathias, but she knows he's among that noisy rabble of teenage exuberance. Mathias is sixteen. She crosses the floor towards a slightly smaller room. The boys seem to be chatting, sitting on the ground in a circle—you need to conquer something these days and the skeleton of this mill is what they have adopted as their own—all five of them jump when they see Julia at the door, then Mathias gets up and pulls her into a third room. This one is really small. The walls are painted light green, there is a pedestal for a kitchen sink and a rectangular table with no chairs. Julia is scared of her brother, she starts to breathe heavily. Three pages torn from a magazine are stuck next to each other on the wall, each showing a full frontal view of a naked woman, one is touching herself between the legs, another is grabbing her own breasts, the third is getting her butt wet in a waterfall. They all have frizzy, voluminous hair and two of them have bangs. It all looks seriously old. They are watching Julia with smiles just like the bad girl's leer.

"What are you doing here? Go away."

"I just came to ask you something."

"Ask me something, are you crazy, can't you do it later when I get home?"

"Did we have a brother?"

Mathias starts to say something, and that something suddenly becomes nothing more than a burst of exhaled air. Then he starts to walk confusedly in all directions, looking at the floor, until he stops in front of the magazine pages. He raises his head and begins to punch the woman in the waterfall furiously, as if it was all her fault. The adhesive tape at one of the upper corners comes away.

"Who told you that, I'm going to crush whoever it was. It could only have been Marcela."

He utters her name through gritted teeth.

"It was her."

"And you still hang out with that deadbeat, I don't understand you. Haven't I told you a thousand times she's a little whore?"

"Did we have a brother?"

Another piece of adhesive tape unsticks, and the woman with her butt in the waterfall gives way to an upside down whiskey advertisement. Mathias rips the page from the wall.

"We did."

"A little boy? Why don't I remember him?"

"He was born and died a few years before you."

Mathias's voice is measured and monotonous, as if he's forcing himself to act like a proper adult, and as if being adult means, among other things, regarding the death of a baby as something entirely everyday. Julia begins to cry, as two of the boys from the other room spy on the scene from afar, not understanding a thing. She wants to go home, but home seems to have become a terrible place too. Her mother's arms have become tentacles. And the constant dizzy spells and Saturday afternoons when mom had to lie in bed and that period when she took leave from the bank and went to Aunt Ana Lúcia's place in Barros Cassal to rest suddenly seem to make more sense. The same goes for her father, shut away in the little room at the back where he makes models out of matchsticks and listens to LPs of gaucho music and doesn't like being interrupted at all. Mathias looks at his sister, still unwilling.

"It's all fine."

"Tell me how he died."

"It was kind of stupid, I think. In a bathtub."

Julia starts sobbing again.

"We had a bathtub?"

"Where our shower cubicle is now."

"Was my room his room then?"

"Come on, Ju, that's enough. We're going home now. Mom'll talk to you herself."

"No, I don't want to go home ever again!"

Her voice echoes through the carcass of the mill and she is somehow frightened by her own presence. She runs out, bumps into something, cries some more, her mom will tend to her cut knees with antiseptic and warm blows before starting to tell her about the accident in the bathtub.

8.

How long had we been sitting like this, one in front of the other? I uncrossed my legs, the one on the bottom had of course gone to sleep. Julia was inspecting her nails. There was a crack in the wall, right behind the sofa, thick like Indian ink, giving the strange impression that it was coming out of the middle of her head. Julia used one nail to push back the cuticle of another. She moved slightly to one side, the crack lost its meaning, I stood up.

"I'm going to brew up some maté, okay."

The bag issued a generous cascade of *erva-mate*, and a cloud of dust enveloped the gourd before finally settling, partly inside, partly on the counter. I filled the kettle with water, the smell had never been one of the best, I looked for the lighter, turned on the gas, a click, and the flame drew an ancestral circle.

Julia was at the door. She looked like she had just woken from a siesta as long as a night's sleep.

"Are you tired?"

"A bit. Can you tell?"

She shuffled over to the table and stood there, playing with the lid of the thermos. After a while, the kettle began to make a slight noise. I turned off the flame and asked what had happened in the bathtub before she was born. She turned to face me with an oh-so-we're-still-talking-about-this expression, and said that he had simply drowned, his mother left the room for a second, the faucet was running, a few inches of water perhaps, he must have fallen in and couldn't turn over. I thought about insects that wind up with their feet in the air and can only hope for some kind of miracle to release them from that position, as ridiculous to us as it is fatal to them. I was still preparing the maté. The ground herbs filled just under half the gourd now, and I tipped it to one side to distribute them evenly.

"Do you leave it to settle with hot water?"

"I do."

"Most people do it with cold or tepid, don't they?"

"To be honest, I've never noticed the difference, I think it's mostly gaucho affectation."

I dug in the straw and took the first sip.

"How old was he?"

"Seven months."

"Jesus, seven months."

"I've never seen a photo of him, there are none, not that there was much time for photos. There's one of my mom pregnant and I always thought she was pregnant with me, but when she told me the story she said: that was your brother. There wasn't a date on it. I just can't really think of him like that, as a brother, you know."

"I know."

"I think I see him more as an accident. The accident. Those few seconds that screw up everything that comes after. It took me quite a while to stop feeling like a victim of history, like, okay, you left, now I'm the one who has to get through this shitty childhood and adolescence that's all patched together because no one can face the fact that you died in a stupid situation when they should have been taking care of you. No one takes care of anyone else in that house. And then it's like I've been betrayed—"

"Betrayed?"

"—not just by my parents and Mathias, but by the whole town. *Everyone* knew, Cora."

"You were very young."

Julia said nothing. She took the gourd and poured in the bubbling hot water. The steam danced before disappearing.

"I don't get why you've only told me this now."

She slid her hand over my face, her pinkie catching between my lips, I immediately hooked my finger in a belt loop of her jeans. If there was one thing I loved, it was pulling someone by the belt loops. It was long, like a kiss of reconciliation should be.

"Right," I said when she finished.

She laughed.

"Right what?"

"I want to know what happened with Marcela."

"Marcela. Marcela lives in Porto Alegre, as far as I know. She never apologized and I never saw my plastic vomit again."

"You'd have found out sooner or later."

"I'd just rather it had come from my mom."

In the yard, we spread out a sarong with the same pattern as the cobbled sidewalk at Copacabana and sat on it, passing the maté between us for hours and hours. That afternoon, I felt like I was moving along a strange path of happiness that was too narrow for two people to pass side by side. I had a sudden desire to take to the road, even though we were only supposed to leave the house the following day. I wanted to drive in the dark. I rested my head on Julia's lap, thinking about driving in the dark. I was saying one thing as I visualized something else, which was the countryside, cut down the middle by a dirt track and the barely sufficient glare of my headlights. Then finally I told her that we had to leave that day, as soon as night fell, I would be careful, as long as she let me listen to Bruce Springsteen until we arrived in Bagé, if you really want to, she replied with that little laugh that showed she didn't quite get me, who am I to say no, who am I, it'll be fun, I concluded, it'll be fun, she repeated, but Cora, do we need to run off and pack our things right this minute?

From the yard to the bedroom, Julia in front, me behind. She sat on the bed. She gestured with her hand, I understood that I should stay standing for now. She ordered me to take off my shorts. Jesus, what an evolution, I thought, as I gently forced the fabric over my hips, the shorts slipping to the floor, me stepping out of them. But that wasn't any more revealing than wearing a bathrobe or the kind of old t-shirt you sleep in. She ordered me to take off my top as well. I waited for a second before moving, I looked hard at Julia and she was serious and focused like an employer conducting interviews, in which hypothesis I would be the half-slut half-dancer candidate, proportions under scrutiny, waist, breasts, firmness of glutes, that untamed hair, private pole dance and sofa test. She rotated her finger as if mixing an imaginary drink. I turned round slowly, following her instructions, one foot, then the other, in tiny steps until I was standing with my back to her. I felt my heart pounding. Julia Ceratti, you frisky thing, what's going on in that head of yours, Lady Half-Light, Miss Amethyst 1999, youngest child, room 23 of the Maria Imaculada all-girls residence, very attractive Latina immigrant seeks First World man for serious relationship, occasional lesbian when no one's watching, what is going on in that little head. I felt a kiss at the height of my shoulder blades, then a hand, then they both descended, synchronized and greedily, mouth and hand, they fitted into the curves of my back, they released my panties, proper black panties, they threw me on the proper mattress in that proper house. I began to breathe like an asthmatic.

Before we left the house, we closed all the windows, turned off the gas, disconnected the freezer, folded the sheets, checked the front gate to prevent any stray dog, horse or cow invading the yard, then finally we handed the keys over to the care of the neighbor. A smell of coffee wafted through the door.

"You didn't see the open mine, I can't believe it, the water's so blue, it's beautiful. Why drive by night when you could leave tomorrow morning, hmm?"

"Do you happen to know how long it takes to get to Bagé?"

"About two hours, two and a half. That is, about two and a half for someone who's not used to dirt roads, and at night. After that it's asphalt all the way. Very good asphalt."

On the main street, three cars passed in convoy in the opposite direction to us. The sky was still grasping onto the last rays of light, making the landscape imprecise and rather threatening. Julia was searching for something in her bag. By the Cine Rodeio, a pick-up took the bend wide and entered the street with its headlights glaring. There were about four people in the back. Julia found what she was looking for, a Tylenol, "headache" she said, then tossed the pill into her mouth and took a long slug of water, her neck leaning back exaggeratedly. When the pick-up passed our car, the driver peered in as if he recognized us immediately, whereas I didn't have the slightest idea who he might be. Then, he gave three short beeps. I glanced in the rearview mirror. He had stopped a few yards away. The reverse light came on. "Who is it?" I asked Julia, braking abruptly to wait for him to approach. "I think . . ." The pick-up drew level with us. "Ahem."

"What's up, ladies, where are you heading?"

Lucian's forehead had started to peel. He cranked the window all the way open. In the back of the truck, a woman with frizzy hair and a man with something stuck to his head leaned out to see us.

"We're leaving," I replied.

"Oh, stay longer. If you want to come with us, we're going to the reject right now, there's going to be a fair bit of activity tonight. Urandir has arrived."

"Activity? What, like rock, drugs, summer cocktails?"

He didn't find that funny. He looked at me with a mixture of irritation and embarrassment.

"Like the forty-nine partner races in the project."

"The forty-nine . . . okay. Who's Urandir?"

He laughed, incredulous at such ignorance.

"You don't watch much TV, do you?"

"Not much."

"Have you never heard of the ET Bilu?"

"Unfortunately not. Are he and Urandir the same person?"

"Are you kidding me? Of course not. They communicate."

In the back of the truck, the guy with the thing on his head pressed a button and the thing lighted up, illuminating the interior of our car for a moment. Then darkness again. Julia placed a hand on my leg. That seemed to be her way of showing that we had to be going and, please, don't get involved in any of this mess.

"Good luck with the flashing lights," I retorted before accelerating away.

A road at night in the south of Rio Grande do Sul. A gas station announced itself as the last one for fifty-five miles. Machine mochaccino for two *reais*, pumps with no customers, a lame mongrel pup sticking his muzzle into the discarded remains of a meat pie. A road at night was obscene. White line fever, lunatic truck drivers on their way to Uruguay. It seemed like the right time to leave. I was driving with Bruce Springsteen, three albums and then Bagé. On the face of it, I had the impression that it was a nice town, I had always liked the word Bagé, the merest mention of it sent me into an inexplicable state of excitement. Just don't tell me that Bagé means something like bluebottle in Guarani, I'd rather not know.

The old houses were pleasant, set directly against the street, with no yards or gardens, each one joined to the next, giving a strange notion of continuity that was broken only by the difference in colors. Narrow doors, the occasional ornament, a balcony where the family was slightly more prosperous, and then came the real palaces with a French accent, stained glass windows, pretentious columns, Bagé had once been a town with money. To my surprise, there was quite a lot of activity on the street, cars, people coming out of restaurants or sitting in the square sipping maté, children on swings, and more black people than anywhere else we had passed through. While we took an aimless spin round, just to see how the town presented itself at half ten on a night in late March, I decided that Julia and I should stay in a good hotel, in an excellent hotel, an ostentatious hotel, after all the trip wouldn't last much longer, and with our nights numbered it wasn't a problem if I squandered my scant finances. *Carpe diem.* You never know. Tomorrow is another day.

Julia didn't seem to favor the idea, she was a proud girl, and let's just say that, as we discussed it, I became less sure that it was the right thing to do, I might be accused of following rigid and old-fashioned rules of behavior where you pay everything for the women you're sleeping with; I didn't want to follow those rules, of course not, and in any case I wasn't a man, but the fact that I wasn't a man didn't absolve me, the fact that I wasn't a man wasn't enough to be called a feminist or a democrat or, who knows, a rebel. I was in such a quandary about it all that I almost didn't notice when Julia said: "Obviously I'd love to stay in a cool hotel." With the help of some friendly locals, we got directions to a place in a pretty nineteenth-century mansion. It looked like it came straight out of the pages of a historical family saga; there was an internal courtyard with a pond and an arcade under which you could just imagine the dashing captain wooing a pretty young maiden. Or Zorro drawing his sword.

Contorting herself so that the long ash on her cigarette didn't drop on the floor, Fany, the hotel manager, guided us round enormous ornate halls with heavy, proud furniture; the floors had jaw-dropping geometric designs and the people in the paintings seemed to be aware that they'd be in them for all eternity. Fany, however, ignored all the historic details, as if the place were just another Ibis or Formula 1 on the outskirts of an irrelevant city. That night, she was too worried, because a monkey called Juju had escaped from the enclosure it shared with the peacocks, guinea fowl and other less interesting animals. It would doubtless return when it was hungry, Fany consoled herself, half a banana in her hand, the name Juju repeated in the dark, while her daughter, a little girl of around ten with indigenous features, observed us from a reserved distance.

I felt like the whole mansion belonged to us. A single door was shut. Probably a room occupied by other guests. In ours, there were two rooms, a kind of ante-room and then the bedroom proper, a canopy of carved wood over the bed, nightstands with marble tops, a bureau above which a picture of a saint had been hung. When we were alone, Julia commented that in the olden days people must have been much smaller. That was the conclusion I had come to after seeing narrow and extremely short beds in French castles, which led me to question the concepts of queen size and king size, *that* particular royal family didn't seem to have the slightest bit of interest in spacious mattresses. Too much Coca Cola and chicken packed with hormones, I retorted to Julia. Then I went after the manager.

Of course I could make a collect call, replied Fany. "Dial one for an outside line, okay, dear?" And with that, she turned her back on me, tugging behind her the girl who, without protest, left behind an unfinished drawing and her box of crayons. The drawing showed the mother, Juju and her. I think she still had to create the surroundings, as the two characteristic outlines of tree trunks didn't yet finish in those plump, cushiony tops. The portrait of the three of them, however, seemed to have been completed, the difference between the monkey and the humans being just two rounded ears on top of the head and a tail. Juju was also a couple of inches taller compared to the girl, and a bit shorter than Fany. As strange as it might seem, the monkey was the only figure that had the right to a smile.

I dialed my dad's cell number. The ashtray next to the telephone was overflowing with little tubes of ash, and the smell on the mouthpiece was like a nightclub before the smoking ban. It began to ring. One. Two. Three times. On the fourth ring, he answered.

"Hello?"

"Hi. Were you asleep?"

"Cora?"

"It's me."

"Jesus. Wait a minute."

He was probably moving to another room, and as he did so, a door was shut. He breathed deeply.

"I'm just back from the hospital."

"Yes, of course, I can imagine. And how's João Pedro?"

"He's great. Jaque too, thanks for asking. They're both coming home tomorrow. He's a chubby little thing, my boy. Twenty-one inches and seven pounds three."

"Fantastic. And does he look more like an alien or an angry gnome?"

He thought about it.

"I think he looks a bit like me."

"You can seriously tell that about a newborn? To me they all look like little moles, you know? A bit confused, all wrinkly from the strain and they'd rather not open their eyes to avoid a reality shock, or it could be that, I don't know, they're born with too much skin, and then the skeleton just grows underneath and the skin's made to last a good few months without them needing any more. You're the doctor, you should know what I'm talking about."

"I don't know what you're talking about."

Silence.

"What are you doing down there, Cora?"

"You know where I am?"

"Not if you don't tell me."

"In Bagé. Dad. Remember when you bought that video camera for our trips to Europe? And I kept imagining that from then on we'd have a whole load of family films like you see in American movies, those kids running in the garden and stuff, the moment when someone opens a present, the mom picks up a tray in the kitchen and nods to the camera as she passes, and then the granddad arrives, always in an enormous car and with enormous glasses, that kind of thing. But you only used the camera on that trip. And then at an otorhinolaryngology conference in the interior of Maranhão, if I'm not mistaken, to which you obviously went alone. I was really gutted about that."

"I didn't know all that. Sorry."

"Do you know where those tapes might be?"

"In your mom's house, I think. Yeah. In that closet in the office, maybe."

"Not even she knows what's in there."

He laughed and, surprisingly, it was a friendly laugh. Then it sounded like he had slumped onto a sofa or one of those armchairs that swallow you up and are impossible to get out of. It might seem strange, but I couldn't remember what the furniture in his apartment was like, or how it was arranged. My dad sighed.

"What you did wasn't great, Cora."

"You don't need to tell me that."

"I've been your age and I know that it's really nerve-wracking to be young, we want to suffer less and we just suffer too much, too much. I ran away from home once, did you know?"

"You never told me that."

"At the time, there was a pizzeria in Protásio called Merci. And I fell in love with a waitress there. She was nineteen and I was seventeen, her name was Maria Celeste, my God, the most wonderful face I've ever seen. Celeste, I called her Celeste, had come from the interior to study pharmacology, she was crazy about me too, she lived in a bedsit in Salgado Filho, she worked really hard and never passed the entrance exam. I went to her house all the time, until one day I thought damn it, I don't want to leave, so I packed a bag when your granddad and grandma were out, left a melodramatic note and went to live what I thought was my first true love."

"And then what happened?"

"Ah. I don't think she was as keen on the idea as I was. To tell you the truth, it was a terrible idea. Basically, we argued all the time because she wanted me to get a job so that she could study, but I wanted to be a doctor, so I needed to study a lot too. I went home after three weeks."

"My God, I've never heard that story. And her?"

"Well, she tried the entrance exam again, if I'm not mistaken, she didn't pass and went back to Venâncio Aires. I never heard from her again."

"Maybe you'd find her on Facebook," I joked.

"Maybe. Listen, when are you coming to Porto Alegre, Cora?"

"In about a week, I think, at most."

"Another week of your gaucho tour? Oh well, what can I say?"

"I don't know. Nothing, I don't think."

"How's Julia?"

"She's great."

"I love you, kiddo."

"Me too. Look, I'm going to hang up now. Don't forget to say hi to JP for me, okay? And tell him to wait for me with his eyes open."

The following day had no reason to be a terrible day. We woke up, Julia asked me about the phone call and I told her, I opened the window, the sky was as it always should be in the head of a born optimist, blue with clouds as fine as lacework, I stood watching for a while as she got up to go to the bathroom, "I still can't believe the size of this," she shouted from inside, the bathroom was practically the same size as the bedroom, you wondered how many waltzes had been danced in it. Then we walked to the breakfast room, which was in an annex to the main building, from which it was possible to see a swimming pool, cloudy with too much chlorine. The dirty crockery at one of the tables revealed that three guests had passed through, earlier risers than us. The clean place settings for Julia and me completed the headcount: there were only five of us in the hotel. The food was strictly counted like the cups and plates, one slice of ham and one of cheese each, two bread rolls, a hunk of butter, a couple of pots of jelly. Our good mood meant that we didn't mind.

The day was still giving no clues as to the fact that it would be a terrible one. Fany and her daughter were still after the monkey, and they called us when it appeared at the top of a tree near the enclosure. But Juju didn't want to come down. Fany had a banana in one hand again and a lighted cigarette in the other. She barely ever took a puff. I asked what kind of monkey it was and for the first time I heard the girl's voice. "Capuchin," she said. The four of us stared at the treetop for a long time, Juju merely a dark stain among the branches, I wasn't entirely sure that I was actually seeing a monkey, perhaps I believed it more because of the banana than because of the blurry form up above. A man in a hat appeared. He left the engine of his pick-up running, said good morning to Julia and me in a subdued fashion, then again more enthusiastically to Fany and her daughter. "Escaped again?" Yes, we said in unison, he shook his head as if there were no solution and, dramatically changing the subject, he asked Fany if he could borrow a bit of water. I find it funny when people use the word 'borrow' without the slightest intention of returning whatever it is they supposedly have on loan. In any case, I'd rather not be given back a basin of dirty water. As soon as he left with a couple of gallons, Fany told us that there had been severe rationing in Bagé since January because the Sanga Rasa dam was at lower than normal levels and all the surrounding streams were in a pitiful state, full of loose earth, trickles of water than wouldn't sate the thirst of the scrawniest ox on the pampa, so that half the city had their supply cut off between three in the afternoon and three in the morning, after which it was the other half who suffered for the next twelve hours. In the hotel, however, water spilled from the faucets twenty-four hours a day and in abundance, something about the water table, an artesian well and other practices which sounded about as legal as keeping a monkey in captivity.

Fany sighed. "We're tired of not being able to leave here, aren't we, honey?" she said, running her fingers through her daughter's hair, the girl limiting herself to a nod of the head. I didn't immediately understand what that had to do with the lack of water, or rather, the fact that, unlike the rest of the town, there was water here all the time—was such a privilege in fact a constant risk, might people arrive with a stock of empty containers and leave with them full without even asking? Fany laughed, the first time since the previous evening and, astonishingly, she raised the cigarette to her mouth and took a drag. The hotel owner had gone to Porto Alegre, so Fany couldn't leave the mansion until she returned. Don't leave the building. Take care of the building. It seemed a bit extreme.

"If you need something, anything, we can get it for you," said Julia suddenly, looking at the daughter, but addressing the mother. Julia had been quiet for a while. Fany shook her hair loose and re-did her ponytail pulling it even tighter. "You two are sweethearts." That was all she said before moving away with the girl.

It wasn't even one of those days that start off unsettled. We visited the Dom Diogo de Souza museum, which until the end of the 90s housed a fragment of the moon, a gift from Nixon to Médici. The former military dictator Emílio Garrastazu Médici was, unfortunately, a gaucho from Bagé. Then the Pedro Osório palace. The Municipal Institute of Fine Arts. The Pedro Wayne

House of Culture. A cream donut in Padaria Moderna. Julia taking photos crouched on the cobblestones, saying that this place was a nice surprise. Black men in berets and neckerchiefs. Good weather, a fresh breeze, who knows, it might have been the cold *minuano*. We discovered that *correarias* were houses selling gaucho products. They smelled of leather. I bought a pair of espadrilles in the first. In the second, I realized that the fake project I had described to my father, that collection of clothes with a gaucho influence, didn't seem so bad, I'd even go so far as to say that it began to take on a very personal meaning, of course, why not, I could always present it for some module of the course when I had the opportunity, so I decided to fill a bag with all sorts of accessories and took a pair of size 40 *bombachas* thinking about using them as a model in the future. Afterwards, we went to the old workers' village at the Santa Thereza dried meat factory, where we crossed railroad tracks feeling like we were anywhere but Brazil. How many railroads still existed in the whole country? Near the tracks, in addition to the tallest palm trees I'd ever seen, there was a ruined villa covered in graffiti. A group of boys and girls in their early twenties was positioned in an opening, feet dangling in the air, probably in anticipation of the sun setting over the countryside. It would still be a while. In the meantime, they told stories and laughed. The south of the state was a ruin that refused to go completely to the dogs. Strange as it might seem, I felt a certain solidarity and, more than anything, comfortable in the midst of that decay. We returned to the hotel to brew a maté.

It seemed as though the ideal place to stay and drink our maté for what was left of the evening was a kind of island in the artificial lake at the hotel, where the presence of at least two elements made it a picturesque and almost incomprehensible scene: a bare tree with twisted, black branches, as if it had been struck by lightning long ago; and a cave that was clearly fake, concrete molded to look like an organic form that only nature could have created, two openings, a staircase running down the side, which reminded me of Marie Antoinette when she wanted to play at being a peasant in the middle of the domain of Versailles. Out of place, like Marie Antoinette's little hamlet.

Julia let the maté rumble away, as custom dictated. She picked up the thermos to pour me another gourd. When she stretched out her arm, the gourd now full in her hand, I leaned in and tried to kiss her. Try wouldn't be the first word I'd use because to me there was nothing to conquer, it was a kiss that was already won, an obvious kiss, a logical kiss, a kiss that was less discovery and more continuation. Julia, however, chose to shrink from it, turning her face at the last second, and suddenly the word *humiliated* lighted up in neon above my head. I stared straight ahead, more to avoid Julia than seeking any reason for her rejection. Fany and her daughter were hurrying under the arcades. I realized what had just happened.

"You shouldn't have done that," I said.

"Sorry."

"It isn't great knowing that you're ashamed of me."

"Cora, it isn't a question of shame. But why would you put a mother in a situation like that, having to explain to her daughter why sometimes two . . ."

"Having to explain to her daughter how the world works? I thought that's what mothers did."

She didn't reply.

"I thought you'd got over your, what should I call them, your moral issues."

Fany had disappeared by now. Julia breathed deeply. I thought for a moment about that group of friends waiting for the sunset. They were laughing inside my head, their legs swinging crazily on the second story of the ruined villa.

"Why did you never introduce me to your parents?"

"They lived in another city."

"So? Your dad used to go to Porto Alegre sometimes, your brother too, but something always happened and I ended up never meeting them, even though we were together almost all the time back then, you must have noticed, isn't it strange? I always found it really strange. And then you could have invited me to Soledade with you some time."

"You would have thought them all idiots, and they would have thought you were crazy. It made no sense."

"Wait a minute. Are you admitting that you wanted to keep things separate?"

"Where's the advantage in mixing them, Cora?"

Now that I had begun, I felt that I had to finish in some way. Finishing, in arguments of this kind, generally means going round in useless circles until someone gets tired. So I pushed the matter. Apart from anything else, I was speechless about the idea that Julia's family would take me for crazy if we had ever been introduced. The funny thing was that deep down I wanted to come across as a bit of a kook, I always made a point of seeming that way, and yet if someone called me that—look at that screwball across the street!—of course I'd be offended. And so the conversation took an unexpected turn. If you had asked me, I couldn't have said that I noticed any of this happening, a change in tone of voice, facial movements, an uncontrollable desire to talk, I mean, everything must have been signaling an imminent fight, but I missed the warnings, like someone who prefers the sea on a red flag day. Avoiding complications was no longer an option, and on that bench next to the fake cave I allowed the atmosphere to get angry and probably deserved every blow I was receiving.

"You really wanna know? Sometimes I think you're just using me as a trophy. Or to prove your wonderful superwoman theory."

"What superwoman? I don't have any such theory. And even if I knew what superwoman meant, Julia, have you ever heard me talk about that?"

"You think we're so hot, don't you? We're hot."

"Yes."

"It's so obvious. If you could see how you act with the people we meet, my God, you wear your superiority like a badge. Civilization visits barbarity. Like we're civilization. The two of us. Together."

"I don't see what that has to do with being hot."

"Civilization, beauty, the right clothes. The right bands. You got a girl and you are a girl, neither of us even close to what you'd expect from girls who go with girls, aesthetically speaking. Which proves that they're all wrong and that you get so much more out of everything. You need to *show* that, basically, because if you can't then it's no fun. It's the only way for them to understand that their preconception needs to move on, preferably to be switched for *your* ideals."

"Hmm. I don't know what to tell you. It sounds like a good argument, at least."

"You know I'm right."

"I don't think you're right. Not much anyway. Right. Perhaps you are."

She smiled, partly disappointed in me, partly satisfied at the victory. As for me, I felt a terrible mess. I hadn't even been able to try to formulate a comeback, why did I put my points across so early, I wondered, shouldn't I have at least held back a bit? Julia stood up. I asked where she was going. She said she wanted to be alone for a while, she turned her back and then took an eternity to enter the hotel, or so it seemed to me because I didn't take my eyes off her the entire time. She didn't look back once. The night sort of contracted over my head. This would be the part of the movie where "The Rain Song" would be playing in the background, you'd see me sitting on that bench for long enough to understand that I was really suffering, it was a Led Zeppelin song, from that album that Julia and I had listened to so often in the Maria Imaculada, a few retrospective scenes would attempt to portray the countless situations I was keeping warm in my memory, her dancing on the Bertussi Memorial, me opening the wine bottle with my boot, her with her feet on the chenille bedspread, the two of us at the canyons with Beto and Petal, the kiss in the toilets at the rest stop, a dirt track whose ruts launched us into giggles, removing panties in haste during those lazy afternoons in Minas do Camaquã. But then we'd unfortunately have to return to reality, to my sad face contemplating the ground, and, soon afterwards, as if responding to the most dramatic part of the song, which rocks everything for five minutes and calms down again with no great traumas, there I am raising my head, not clutching at some kind of ray of optimism or dignity, but because I've just seen some headlights, car headlights, my car's headlights passing through the gate and then vanishing.

There isn't even time to react. I leave the island slowly. A puppy barks nearby. We are separated only by an almost invisible electric fence behind a pile of bamboo canes, like the kind we used to play with on the street. The neighbor was soft on us, all threat and no action. This was long before I'd chosen Courtney Love as a private sex symbol and a prime example of a strong woman after her brief appearance at the MTV Music Awards, don't ask me the year, she wore black leather pants. Bamboo canes dated from the uncomplicated part of my life. Courtney Love inaugurated the drama.

For the next hour or more, I wander aimlessly around the hotel grounds. I find the glow from Fany's window. They are watching television. The girl probably doesn't even remember having seen two female guests very close to a kiss in the place where she usually plays. The windows of the other three guests are also lighted up. I find the dark window of our empty room. As I follow a gravel path that leads me to a kind of function suite, I sketch out a weak theory in respect of Julia and me.

At that precise moment, ignoring the fact that there might be differences in our expectations or the enthusiasm of each of us for the other, I could sum everything up in a simple conflict between hiding and revealing. Yes, it made sense, I did want to show her off as some grand prize, a trophy, if those were the words put in my mouth, but that happened precisely because she had been rather difficult to win, and precisely because winning was all I'd wanted over the last few weeks. Anyway, I would admit that part of me delighted in confusing others. It was my teenage rebel side that still hadn't completely disappeared. Another much bigger side, however, was just aiming to have a normal life. That included public displays of affection. Who could blame me?

Following that logic, the real character failing wasn't mine, but Julia's; while I wanted to show her off (ergo, I felt proud of her), Julia preferred to keep me hidden (ergo, she was ashamed of me). Retracing the reasons for that shame was, at this stage, pointless. It didn't matter whether it was the way she was brought up, or how much time she had had to spend in church on Sundays, or whether her romantic ideal had formulated and remained unaltered since the first Barbie and the first Ken. None of that changed the fact that, to all intents and purposes, even though she pushed me between her legs, dug her nails into me, shouted, and laid her head on my stomach afterwards, we were still just good friends.

When Julia returned to the hotel, I was sitting near the enclosure. She stopped the car. With the engine still running, she got out. She left the door open. She walked round to the other side and opened the passenger door wide as well. She held a plastic bag in her hand. "I brought you food," she said. I didn't mention a single word of my theory.

9.

THE ARCHWAY HAD LOST ITS *A*. That was the first thing we saw. On the right-hand side of the highway, which carried on through the arch, there was a basalt walkway, blackened by traffic. People would stroll and run there when the sun was going down. The town itself didn't appear for a while. A cheap hotel. Woods. The coach station. Woods. A billboard in pieces. More woods. The precious stone firms were housed in large concrete boxes like any other factories, a few cars parked outside and no interest in displaying their wares. They were called V. Lodi Cristais, Legep Mineração Limitada, Colgemas Pedras Preciosas, MR Lodi Stone. No sign of any sculpted macaws, phallic amethysts, or agate ashtrays.

The urban sprawl became more evident with the sudden appearance of new-and-used car forecourts, mechanics' workshops, a gas station and suppliers of motor parts. Everything made too much sense and could be summed up in cars and stones. When Julia told me to turn left just after the square, I did as she asked.

"Where's your house? I wanted to see."

"We'll pass it later."

The street climbed, then started to drop again. In the dis-

tance, I could already make out white wall and the two inevi-
tably tall trees that tend to guard the entrance to cemeteries.
They weren't cypresses. The edge of town was close, right behind us, hills as green as golf courses. I stopped the car.

"Look . . ."

"I want to go in. If you don't, wait for me here."

"I'm coming too," I replied.

She didn't move. Two girls in shorts passed in front of the
windshield, they looked inside, they didn't recognize either of
us and continued walking.

"Have you been here before?"

"No. Did you know that on the local radio every day they
read out the names of everyone who was admitted and dis-
charged from hospital?"

"Should that be, well, allowed?"

Julia thought for a moment, shrugged, and got out.

I must have taken a few seconds to do the same, because
right then I heard a van with a loud hailer, coming ever closer,
I turned to see what it was, it was decorated all over and the
exhausted recording was announcing a circus that night and
the following evenings. The kombi's window cut through the
clown's face, it was open and I doubted whether it would even
shut properly. I saw the driver sucking on a cigarette, he was
looking towards me. As if one thing was leading to the next,
he took one more long drag, still staring at me, before flicking away the butt. I walked to the cemetery. Julia was going
into the administrative office. I thought it would be sensible
to keep my distance, so I did what everyone does in a place
like this: first, I felt rather helpless and fragile and aware of
my own expiration, looking at the collection of tombs which

formed a kind of skyline in a city of the dead, not wanting to imagine what was happening and, more importantly, what was not happening, beneath my boots. So a distraction was needed. The next stage consisted of exactly that, clearing the bad thoughts from my head, which I did by walking, reading the series of inscriptions, inspecting the oval photographs, peering through the dirty glass of the centenarian mausoleums, and, when the second date minus the first date came to anything less than seventy, trying to imagine what on earth had happened to the poor individual to have lived so little. It seems strange, but, after the initial impact, I think that the death of other people makes us think less about our own, that silence, those stones, all those frozen faces were effectively saying that we were alive, that we were going to walk out of there, there was still plenty of time to die.

Julia appeared at my side.

"Come on."

"Where?"

"He told me where the grave is."

"Who did?"

"The gravedigger. Is there a nicer name for that?"

"Not that I know of."

The stone paths became muddled until they finally disappeared, and after that it was inevitable that we would occasionally stand on the edges of other graves as we moved forward. There must have been a strong storm in Soledade that week because artificial flowers were scattered everywhere, honoring the memory of no one in particular. Some red earth had spilled from a slope in the ground, staining the surrounds to the recently built mausoleums, which looked more like a parcel of the federal government's low-cost housing. Julia stopped. We had found her brother's grave. It was next to a smiling lady who had a long life. No flowers. Light marble. The dates almost coincided: M 04-12-1980 > 23-07-198*1*. *Missed by all who love you, mom, dad, brother, aunts and uncles, grandparents, cousins. God is with you.* The dead brother had been called Juliano Ceratti.

Juliano. That left me speechless. After a tragedy of that immensity, they couldn't have done anything more disrespectful to Julia than to baptize her Julia, out of all the popular names of the 80s, Fernanda, Mariana, Tatiana, Taís, Camila, Carolina, Daniela, Laura, Gabriela, Paula, Andréa, Luciana, Alessandra, Flávia. I didn't know her parents, but now I was sure they were the most mistaken people on the planet, and I began to feel really sorry for Julia, as well as having an irresistible urge to explain her entire personality based on what had already been decided before she was born. If she had been called, let's say, Roberta, would she be quite so concerned with always going in a straight line, or rather, maintaining the appearance of someone who always goes in a straight line and never wavers? Would our own story have been any different? I looked at Julia. I think she was praying. Would Roberta pray too? No, not Roberta.

"His name was Juliano," I interrupted. Julia opened her eyes.

"Uh-huh. Didn't I tell you that?"

"No. When did you find out?"

"The same day as everything else, Mathias, he told me when we were still in the mill. It was really bizarre. I stopped writing my name on my schoolwork."

"Seriously?"

"The teacher knew when we handed it in that the one without a name could only be mine, but she was getting a bit worried about it and called my parents for a chat." Then Julia laughed, as if it had done no more harm than that and was just another story in the family folklore.

"The first person you introduce me to is your dead brother. It's probably best I don't think too much about what that means."

"Tomorrow we'll go and look up Mathias."

"Yes, Mathias. Where is he?"

"Don't be difficult, Cora. He and his wife bought a plot in a place called Margem São Bento, it's in the middle of Soledade. How are you finding my native town?

"Ugly as sin."

We laughed for a while. When we left the cemetery, a fine drizzle had started to fall. I smelled that pleasing aroma of wet earth as we walked to the car in no particular hurry. You could tell the difference between the poor houses and the middle-class houses because the poor ones had goats, hens and sometimes a few ears of corn growing in the yard. We got into the car, Julia looked in every direction, no one, no one, no one, no one, then she leaned over the gear shift and gave me a kiss. Then I asked, "Everything okay?" and she replied, head in the clouds, "Fine, Cora, of course it's all fine."

I drove two blocks to a hotel. We had to cross a long, wide corridor before reaching reception. On the right-hand side, there was a collection of display cases showing precious stones in a variety of formats, discs, pyramids, spheres, necklaces, bracelets. On the left-hand side was the entrance to the snack bar (chairs stacked up, I don't they ever left that position) and at least three lounges with 1970s furniture that seemed genuinely hurt at the lack of use it was getting. In the spaces between the glass doors, there were also vinyl armchairs with visible rivets and the final, dated touch was provided by some ashtrays with little feet. In the event that one day the hotel was filled to its maximum capacity, which seemed as remote in the past as in the future, and assuming that all the guests suddenly felt the urge to sit somewhere other than their rooms, they could all be catered for quite comfortably; as we would see shortly, even the upper floors had their quota of useless lounges and colonial benches turned to face the walls.

The man on reception looked like a lunatic. His eyes were open too wide, and his haircut, which seemed to have been molded in a potty, gave him something of the appearance of a gunman in a high school massacre. He wore a shirt with the name of the hotel embroidered on it, his scrawniness making the sleeves unintentionally baggy. I filled out the form. He looked at Julia insistently. I wasn't sure what to write in the *next destination* field. Julia turned to the side, obviously embarrassed. I left it blank. He said: "Sorry to ask, but aren't you the daughter of the precious stone Cerattis?"

I had a few comments to make about that. For example, how much Julia had grown up and how *different* she seemed, they had gone to the same school; once, at recess, you lent me your pogo ball, he added, as if that was proof of old friendship, and what a pity she couldn't remember it at all. Julia was desperate to get out of the conversation, but the receptionist wouldn't stop talking for a minute. He talked about Julia's family. He knew that Ceratti and his wife had moved to a house at the beach, that she had gone to study abroad, where was it again? He wished he could go somewhere far away from here too, Soledade was the wild west now, one of the Lodi family was almost kidnapped, a boy was knifed seven times coming out of a dance because he was messing with someone's wife, two cars with Novo Hamburgo plates blew up a Sicredi branch, kids of fifteen, all of them, were falling into drink and drugs.

An hour later, we were on our way to Julia's house. Her aunt lived there now. She never had children. She had a second husband. Julia squealed when we pulled up in front of the house. She said: "I don't believe this." She didn't believe whatever it was to such an extent that she repeated herself three times. One of those times, she clamped her hand to her forehead, shut her eyes and seemed to hope that she would see something different when she opened them again. It didn't work. She was still devastated. I asked what the problem was. "Can't you see? My idiot of an aunt has gone and painted the house purple!" Of course I'd noticed, but there was no way I could have immediately attributed it to her idiot aunt's bad taste, after all, it was the first time I'd even seen the Ceratti house, where her baby brother had drowned, where Julia was born, where twelve years later a piece of plastic vomit was pilfered from a toy box so that the whole story could come to light. No one in Canada would paint a house purple, Julia was saying, no one, purple simply isn't an option for painting a goddam house. As for France, could I imagine something like this happening in some godforsaken hole in France? Of course not. Never in France, I replied, without really thinking. She seemed relieved.

• • •

He had bought a twelve-acre plot in Margem São Bento, don't ask me how big an acre is, twelve of them were enough for a large house, the two cars, a kitchen garden and his own little piece of native woodland. I'd say he was expecting us. He was sitting in front of the house drinking maté in a plastic chair, the kind that look like bar chairs sponsored by beer brands, but without the beer logo, or the color, without the night all around, the babble, the friends. He could have been sitting there for a long time, that was my first impression, there was something of a tireless guardian about him, a stubborn man, there was no way he was on his first thermos, the day had dawned and he was already there. The kind of guy who often saw the sun take its first peek above the horizon. The gravel driveway came to an end. Julia told me to park where I liked. We slammed the car doors. Mathias made the straw gurgle.

He stared at us as he tilted the thermos and topped himself up. He knew exactly how long it took for the water to reach the usual level, slightly below the mound of *erva-mate*, then he waited the requisite few seconds, set the thermos straight, screwed on the lid and put it on the ground. Then, he very carefully ran his finger over the green surface in the gourd, gently encouraging a fine layer of the herb down into in the steaming water. He didn't say a word during the entire process. His mouth searched for the straw.

It had been more than two years since they had seen each other. From inside the house came the sound of a TV, the hammering, crashing and giggles of cartoons, which made me think for a moment that there were children in the living room, but no, there couldn't have been a child, Mathias wasn't a father yet, Julia had never spoken of nieces or nephews, I simply had to accept the fact that some adults still entertained themselves watching old episodes of Woody Woodpecker. Julia stopped in front of her brother. I lingered a step behind. Mathias was almost blond, his cheeks wounded in the pursuit of a perfect shave. By my calculations, he was twenty-nine now, although having to take care of other people's soya had clearly taken its toll.

"You don't seem very surprised."

"Auntie phoned me yesterday."

"Oh."

"What exactly are you doing here?"

"I don't know. We were passing, we . . . were around. Seeing some places. This is Cora."

"Hi," he said, without paying me much attention.

"I think I've told you about her."

"You haven't seen mom and dad yet?"

"I'm going there tomorrow, maybe. Hey, what's the deal with our aunt painting the house purple?"

He coughed, surprised by a curt laugh.

"You're being sentimental. It isn't our house any more."

"Can I have some maté?"

He opened the thermos. The water burbled. As I was superfluous to the conversation, I tried to look around me and feign some interest in the landscape, but it was as monotonous as the paintings sold at a craft fair. Soya and more soya as far as the eye could see.

"But purple is ridiculous, isn't it. It could be, I don't know, a salmon color? That beige was too discreet for our aunt, I know, she does like those enormous necklaces with dyed agate. And her bedroom, my God!"

Julia grasped the gourd and took her first sip.

"This here is my house. Your house is in Montreal. Mom and dad's house is now . . ."

"Okay, Mathias, I get it."

When I remembered that it was my fault in a way that the two of us were here, out of some kind of moral obligation from our college days, a belated proof that there was nothing to hide from one side (me) or the other (family), regardless, when I remembered that we had driven nearly two hundred and fifty miles to see a grave, a house, an aggressive brother, a town where every corner reaffirmed its deplorable condition, and that none of this would relieve the weight of our personal problems, that none of this would make us happier, that none of this would postpone the end of our trip, the imminent separation, whether we liked it or not, I felt like disappearing.

Time dragged in Margem São Bento. We stayed at the back of the house, slumped in two reclining chairs. Not a hint of a breeze. The immense parasol stretched out a tolerable shadow in the exact space occupied by our chairs. Moving our feet just a couple of inches would plunge us into another temperature zone. If we happened to look behind, we would see Gisele, Mathias's wife, chopping onions, garlic and cabbage for our lunch. Our proximity to the kitchen window was probably what kept our mouths shut. Mathias had gone to sort out a few things on a nearby hacienda, and sorting things out meant giving a lot of care and attention to hundreds of acres of soya. If there are two kinds of plant that have come to symbolize supreme evil in Rio Grande do Sul in recent decades, they are without a shadow of a doubt eucalyptus and soya. Eucalyptus, that withered tree that someone decided to import from Australia and treat as if it was native. Any smallholder or environmentalist could tell you a lot about the spirit of domination and extermination contained within the deep roots of a single eucalyptus. I had often heard about that. And as for soya, suffice it to say that it made the words Monsanto and monoculture instantly spring to mind. No one with a free spirit would believe in things like Monsanto and monoculture.

When Mathias returned, the stew was smelling good, the wife was smiling and the table was set. He asked Julia if she had looked in on Tempestade, he was blind in one eye now, but still happy. Julia replied with an uninterested yes, a very brief spasm of sympathy flitted across her face, then she said, "Is there any *farofa*?" and Gisele ran to the kitchen berating herself for forgetting the traditional accompaniment. The submissive wife embraces any blame without hesitation. The miracle was that Tempestade was still alive, Mathias was saying as he piled a mountain of food onto his plate, remember when he was run over twice in three weeks by Renato Colnaghi's dad? Julia smiled shyly and buried her face in her plate as if thinking: not that story again! Then, before I realized what I was about to do, I let out a shrill giggle and asked Mathias to please tell me what happened.

It was the first time he had spoken directly to me, and I confess that it made me feel good, even though the fact that I was his audience was nothing more than circumstantial; after all I was the only person at the table who had never heard about the two unfortunate accidents, Tempestade's bravery as he lay maimed in the middle of the tarmac, the heavy rain that was falling (those nights that, on their own, produce more than the average rainfall predicted for the entire month), Renato Colnaghi's dad covering his son's eyes and shouting: "It was just an accident! It was just an accident!" But Mathias fell far short of Julia when it came to telling stories. Firstly, he emphasized irrelevant details. Secondly, he interrupted the dramatic parts with lengthy parentheses, the function of which seemed to be merely to destroy our presumed interest in the main story. Finally, and always an indication of failure: he, the narrator, laughed much more than any of those listening to him.

The legendary tales about the little dog Tempestade, however, didn't lead Mathias and I to establish anything more than a temporary communion. Over dessert, he looked at me and seemed suddenly shocked to find sitting in his dining room a girl with dyed hair, black eyeliner, and visible bra straps, who must surely have reminded him of some little whore you'd pick up on an empty road in the middle of the desert, a cross between an almost perfect crime and a vague feeling of freedom. Why did Julia insist on going about with someone who had nothing good to offer? The sago balls were not well cooked. They clung to the depressions in my molars, I needed to poke around with the tip of my tongue with my mouth closed, holding that pose while the other three chatted. Tempestade barked because a cockerel crowed near by. Julia hadn't seen Tempestade and his blind eye at all. At no point had we left those reclining chairs.

"We went to look for Juliano yesterday."

"Juliano who?"

"Our brother, Mathias."

His spoon remained suspended in the air.

"Hang on. You were in the cemetery looking for some fucking grave?"

Julia began to bite the cuticle of her middle finger.

"Have you seen it?"

"Yes, I've seen it. So?"

"Don't you think that, deep down, mom and dad moved away because of it?"

"Don't you think this is kind of something for family only?"

"You mean Gisele and Cora should leave the room for us to continue? Oh Mathias, just stop it."

"What? For God's sake, Gisele is my wife, Julia, you've known her ten years. We're married, there was a party, you were there, you drank too much, you even danced to I don't know what song with Renato Colnaghi, then you came up to me and said that the decorations, that our decorations, seemed, what was it? Tacky."

"I know."

"She *is* family."

"I told Cora about Juliano."

"Listen . . ." I said.

"It's fine, Cora, stay there. I told Cora about Juliano and I don't know why it took me so long to do it."

Gisele looked like a very tired living statue. Standing at the same crossroads every day. She was looking down. In front of her, the sago and the cream had turned into a single, sticky mauve substance with little balls sitting in it. I tried to leave a few times. Julia stretched out her arm to keep me there. The first time, Mathias was saying that it had been a stupid idea to pay for accommodation in Villablanca when practically her whole goddamn family lived there, uncles, aunts, cousins, his own house with two huge rooms that weren't in use, so that everyone would go thinking they weren't good enough for her or something much worse than that. Or something much worse than that. The second time, it had all begun with Mathias accusing Julia of acting like a teenager, and seemingly there's no greater offense among human beings than that, so Julia completely lost her calm and began a ranting counter-argument along the lines of I've-been-getting-by-on-my-own-for-a-long-time-now, for example I pay three times what any other Canadian pays to study because I'm foreign, for fuck's sake. I tried to stand up. She grabbed my hand and said, "Cora." What exactly was my closed mouth needed for? I sat down again. Gisele finished her sago. "Studying," Mathias was saying. "That's *exactly* what I'm talking about! How old are you, Julia, shouldn't you be qualified for something, anything?"

That was the third time.

"Seriously, I'm going."

I got up from the table, tripped over a rug, caught a glimpse of a wedding photo above the fireplace, I thought I was going to fall, as well as a photo of Gisele looking very young wearing a woolen hat, a framed agronomy diploma, I tried to pretend nothing was happening, but I trod so heavily towards the door that it must have seemed like I wanted to crush something. That wasn't entirely untrue.

Outside, I leaned against the car for a good few minutes, looking at Mathias's house. Nothing moved. The house stayed the same. The door stayed the same. I got into the car, reclined the seat and, in that moment, almost forgot to wait. I closed my eyes. The only information that remained was that I was somewhere light. For some strange reason, disconnected images from the streets of Paris began to flit across my mind, as if I was in the middle of the street, as if I was lying in the center of the asphalt on a day with no cars, the rigid lines of buildings on either side, wrought iron balconies, an open window in the slate roof, a girl watering a single flowerpot, it made me think how lucky it was to see such a sunny day in Paris, the tiny clouds beginning their long and tiring journey to the other side of La Mancha, even though just focusing on those small clouds gave me vertigo.

The door slammed. Julia was crying, her face turned away in unnecessary shame. "Can we go already?" She sniffed before saying that, she sniffed afterwards, I found a paper tissue from somewhere, I turned on the engine and moved off hesitantly down the street. Soya and more soya all around.

Julia was asleep now. I wasn't. I had closed the door carefully, as if I had just finished reading a bedtime story, a long, relentless, soporific one. I had crossed the rough corridor in socks, gone downstairs, asked the weirdo at reception for a cigarette, felt his eyes glued to my back on that long walk to the hotel entrance, the way I moved, my hair tangled back with an elastic band that had been forgotten somewhere, the indecent sleep shorts, a pit of worry. I sat outside on the edge of a flowerbed and lighted the cigarette with the match the weirdo had also offered me.

The glowing ember might have seemed nice on that empty, desperate night in Soledade, but it was only the third time in my life I had smoked tobacco, so I recall having coughed repeatedly until I convinced myself that my throat wasn't ready for long drags, after which the cigarette became less of a chemical comfort and more of an accessory for my fingers, fingers that were very restless in those wee small hours. In the time I spent sitting by the flowerbed, not much happened outside of my head. A cat climbed into a trashcan and came out with its mouth full. On the street behind, someone stuck their head out of their car, shouted *wake up guuuuys*, then stepped on the gas. I occasionally glanced through the glass doors and the hotel reception was almost as dark as the rest of the town, that long, wide corridor slumbering in the insufficient glow of emergency lights, the 1970s furniture fitting in perfectly, much more than it did in the mid-afternoon sun, at any rate.

I thought again about what it would be like to leave suddenly. The idea was tempting, I had already tried it, I had fled my dad's wedding to Jaqueline, I had fled from the birth of my little brother, why not flee too from a goodbye that was only going to be a disaster? It was without doubt the most cowardly of all my options, but, as far as I could tell, what it saved in drama seemed to compensate what it would gain in weight on my conscience. But no. Not this time. I wasn't going to leave a note or something for Julia, get the car out of the hotel garage and drive to Porto Alegre in the middle of the night, that was unthinkable, and not because of some strange calculation in my head, but because a drastic measure like that would bury our chances forever. On the contrary, I wanted to keep building up those chances, until they were more than chances, or more than a heap of ambiguities, more than two rather unstable sexual identities that one day might happen to intersect and produce one of those stories you'll remember your whole life, but which quickly become a kind of recognition that your youth was complete, days that were crazy, sweet and full of adventure—hell, what a phase!—just that, that sweet memory and the conviction that, when it boiled down to it, when that thing that looked very much like love was actually happening, you already knew that recalling it years later would threaten the calm and predictability that were unfortunately part of your destiny. Perhaps that was the purpose of all those confusions.

No. I didn't want any of that to happen to me. My cigarette had become an insignificant stub. I crushed the glowing end on the ground and entered the hotel holding on to that stinking remain. Behind the counter, the weirdo was reading a detective novel. I asked if he had a trashcan and, not waiting for an answer, I placed the stub and the box of matches on the granite surface and went upstairs.

Julia was still asleep. She had rolled into the middle of the bed since my exit, as if no one else was going to lie there that night, her body drawing an uncertain C, the sheet clinging to her like a cocoon. It was stifling in there. The minibar started yet another cycle of hums and hisses. I entered the bathroom and started removing my make-up with one of those cotton wool pads from Julia's toilet kit. I allowed the black to smear across my temples, transforming myself into a cross between a victim of domestic violence and a supermodel addicted to sedatives. I felt like I was stripping myself. I took another cotton pad, a bit of make-up remover, not from my little plastic pot that looked like a free sample, but from Julia's, which had writing in English and French, I rubbed vigorously, across my temples, then across my closed eyelids, then along my lash lines, then I opened the faucet, let the water run as if I were waiting for it to turn into something much more interesting, I thrust my face under the stream which, after all, was the same water as ever, and dried myself with a towel, taking care to switch off the light before opening the door.

Julia moved slowly in the darkness. I stood watching. Her hands found a new resting place under the pillow, then her legs separated in a kind of nightmare spasm to then snap back together as if joined by a pin at the knees. The sheet was long gone. I stayed standing. She opened her eyes. At first, it was impossible to be sure that they were even open, after all I couldn't see a tiny thing like a pair of eyes clearly, or rather, the difference between a pair of closed eyes and a pair of open eyes, so I was only certain that Julia had woken up when she took her arm from under the pillow and, with a single movement, pushed a few troublesome strands of hair off her cheek. After that, I think everything happened rather oddly. She didn't say "hi" or "why are you awake?" or "you should try to get a bit of sleep"; she didn't say anything. She seemed to find it normal that I was wide awake and, worse than that, looking very much like someone who hasn't even been to bed. She straightened the pillow, sat with her legs stretched out and waited. I sat near her, but in the way that people sit when they're about to get up. Did she *have* to go away? I asked in a pleading tone: "Are you really going tomorrow?" Julia gave me the saddest smile in the world.

"My parents. They've been expecting me for a while."

"I know. Your parents."

"We have to please our parents once in a while."

"Mmhm."

Then she made a gesture that was an invitation for me to snuggle into her lap. Lying there, my legs interlaced with hers, her rake-like fingers winning a hard battle with my hair, I wondered whether Julia was in some way trying to console me. As if, hell, I was the only unhappy girl in need of consolation in that depressing hotel room. At some point between my unanswered question and the first rays of sun, we both fell asleep.

The goodbye actually began on the way to the coach station. Once more, the car salesrooms, the mechanics' workshops, the gas station. Julia looked out of the window like someone looking for the last time. I stopped to fuel up, she didn't move. The morning brought with it the promise of a tiresome heat, stray dogs were lying in the shadows of verandas, and a swarm of flies fought for space with the sparrows for a sticky morsel of bread. I stood outside the car while the attendant filled the tank. I thought about how long it would take to get to Porto Alegre, perhaps about four hours, shouldn't I let my mom know that I was finally on my way back? "Miss," someone said. The car key was practically dangling at my nose. "It came to seventy-four twenty." I pulled two notes of fifty out of my pocket, put away the change, shot a have-a-nice-day at the attendant and the other man who had cleaned my windows. There was Julia, in exactly the same goddamn position, so distant and wrapped up in her own dramas that I thought it best to keep my mouth shut. There were the squat factories of the precious stone firms, MR Lodi Stone, Colgemas Pedras Preciosa, Legep Mineração Limitada.

The Soledade coach station could almost have been mistaken for one of those buildings. It was a more precarious version of the same functional architecture, low and square, the only difference being that two sections of the construction appeared to have been removed to facilitate access to the back.

In the parking lot, there were very few cars and no shade. I parked. So this was it. We began the tough job of taking out her bags and leaving mine, going to the ticket office, asking for a single one-way ticket.

"I think I can turn on my cell now," Julia said, still sitting. It was the first smile of the day. She took the device out of her bag, pressed a button, the screen lighted up.

"Do you think Mathias spoke to your parents? I mean, after yesterday afternoon."

She looked at me as if that question was beneath my intelligence.

"Okay, I get it. He likes to give the first version of events."

"Exactly."

There was a short silence. Julia was playing with the Navajo bracelet. I began to speak.

"I just wanted to tell you that all this, the trip, was just, well, incredible."

"It really was, wasn't it?"

Her face lighted up.

"You like this bracelet of mine?"

"Your Navajo bracelet? Of course, it's lovely. I'm sure it was the prettiest thing you could have bought on that reservation. And it makes me think about, I don't know, about the desert. It's like it *brought* the whole desert with it, you know?" I laughed to myself. "Sorry, that was really stupid."

"It wasn't stupid. Look, you have to take it. No, Cora, I mean it. Take my bracelet." She forced the ends over her slim wrist. "I know, it was Eric who gave it to me, so it's kind of a second-hand present. But I think you'll be able to see that in a special way."

"I certainly will."

The bracelet was on my wrist now. Julia began to laugh. At that moment, there was a scatter of bright sparks, lighter than air.

"Aren't we just like a couple of teenagers? Swapping clothes and that kind of thing."

"I . . . Thanks, it's pretty. Really."

And as if there was nothing more to be said, we got out of the car.

While Julia dragged her case towards the only ticket window, glancing up at an old analogical panel full of names of towns and exact timetables, I walked to the back of the coach station. That was where the buses stopped. The backless wooden benches were occupied by all sorts of people and a variety of luggage, including a soft rectangular case that seemed to protect some kind of musical instrument. To my left, there was a bed with a withered palm tree, with more dead leaves than living, struggling to survive. On the opposite side, a Coca Cola mural covered the wall from top to bottom. They don't do paintings like that any more. That must have been several decades ago. Ironically, below the obsolete slogan, an indigenous family had set up camp. At that precise moment, in the midst of the confusion of scattered clothes and grocery carts replete with unidentifiable items, the indigenous woman was feeding three children, none of them more than six or seven years old. The head of the family must have been elsewhere, rummaging through garbage for aluminum cans.

"Ready."

I turned round.

"It leaves at half eleven for Passo Fundo. Then I have to

catch another bus to the Santa Catarina coast. You think my parents will come and get me in, maybe, Camboriú?"

I looked at my watch.

"Forty minutes."

"Yeah. Forty minutes."

When the time came, she embraced me tightly and kissed me on the cheek. 'Take care," she said. And she kept looking back and smiling in that line that never moved forward. The coach's engine seemed to mark the tragic pulse of our goodbye. I looked at the indigenous family, the snack bar, the palm tree. Perhaps I hadn't done enough for Julia to stay. But stay where exactly? Apart from anything else, I needed to leave too. I was going to see my mom, my dad, my little brother, to hear that I'd been a naughty girl, and then catch my flight back to Paris.

Finally, the driver uttered his last unenthusiastic good morning. He ripped Julia's ticket and gestured for her to get on. After that, the tinted windows weren't good enough for final waves, and I don't think I was good enough for them either, I was still thinking I should have done something else, one last thing to prevent her getting on that coach, so that even before the driver began to reverse I was already walking toward the parking lot. It was murderously hot, I had to get used to the blinding light and then to the heat that had been accumulating inside the car, but above all to the empty seat that was now next to me. I turned the key, inspired by the childish idea of driving under the Soledade archway before the coach did. A red car was leaving the parking lot at the same time. I had the impression that I saw Mathias. I was probably wrong again.

10.

FIVE DAYS A WEEK, I worked at Monte Cassino, 76, Avenue des Gobelins. It was a restaurant much like any other Italian restaurant that happened to be on a Parisian corner, the orange awning, the word *pizza* on one side and *trattoria* on the other, Sicilian landscapes in Indian ink, disposable placemats that would be spattered with tomato sauce and red wine by the end of every meal. From the window you could see the uninterrupted carousel of drivers circling Place d'Italie. We were in October, it was raining, and the drops accumulating on the glass deflected yellow and red lights. It wasn't a heavy rain, more like a kind of condensation that was so light it seemed immune to the effects of gravity. The pedestrians ignored it completely.

In October, everyone was still trying to cure their summer hangover. A summer in Paris could be nothing less than memorable. The city was radiant in the sun, as places that don't see it very often tend to be, so that people needed to be out in it the entire time, drops of sweat on the forehead on café terraces, drinking, walking, cycling, having picnics with real picnic hampers and real picnic blankets, which barely resembled the very thin sarongs we used to spread out on Sunday afternoons in

Porto Alegre. I had seen someone with a table on the banks of the Seine. Don't ask me how it got there.

But now the patches of grass in the squares were in their winter repose. For each nice day, there were three as bad as this. Parisians were drying out and losing their leaves. At the Vélib' station, a Rastafarian released a bicycle from the far left-hand side of the stand with a brusque tug, placed his rucksack in the basket and pedaled off without even acknowledging the drizzle. Surely that had to be one of the definitions of a European: someone who isn't bothered by going out in the rain.

I stopped watching and turned back to the dining room. Romantic Italian hits were still trickling through the sound system. There was my boss, counting money. I would never know whether the fact that he had dark, slicked-back hair had had anything to do with him being hired, or whether his Mafioso air was constructed and refined *a posteriori*. There was the table whose occupants, two tourist couples from Eastern Europe, seemed to have nothing to say to one another, except when the youngest man sneezed, which happened fairly frequently; then the others quickly said whatever it was polite to say in their country under such circumstances. There was the guy who had never seen an egg on a pizza. He was eating tiramisu now, the kind that was delivered twice a week in a refrigerated truck. In front of him was an open book lying spine up, like a musty tent. A seriously old volume. Finally, there were the only French folk in the premises, a man and a woman who seemed to have come straight from a business meeting. The man wanted to continue the meeting, unlike the woman, who limited herself to shaking her head at her companion's excited torrent of ideas, occasionally reaching the point of shutting her eyes between words. She alone had finished the half-liter carafe of red wine. Her hair, scraped back in a ponytail, gave the impression that it had been sculpted in a single automatic gesture that simultaneously took into account its importance in the balance of her face. That was one of the potential definitions of a Frenchwoman: someone who ties back her hair with calculated discipline.

The fine rain lingered when we closed the restaurant.

Every night, I walked home, covering part of Boulevard Auguste Blanqui, then climbing Rue des Cinq Diamants from beginning to end, one, two, three blocks that became progressively smaller, until I came out in what was without doubt my favorite part of the journey, the lively and semi-isolated hub of a district known as Quartier de la Butte aux Cailles. This pretty hill was a kind of small-scale Montmartre where tourists never went, and because there were no tourists, no guy from Mali would try to tie a colored cord round your wrist and then demand some small change in return for the charming souvenir. I cut across a triangular square, someone was smoking a cigarette and talking on the telephone in spite of the lacework of raindrops in the air, I turned left into Rue Barrault, then left again onto Daviel. In this area, there were two architectural curiosities that seemed to be mandatory in tourist guides with names like *Hidden Paris* or *Unexpected Paris*. The first of these distinctive edifices was a complex of Alsace-style buildings. Dramatic roofs like you would imagine a witch's house to have, surrounded a leafy courtyard. Often, immediately after one of the residents walked out, someone would grab the still-closing gate and sneak in to have a quick look. Even I had done that. The second oddity was called Villa Daviel. Villa Daviel was basically a cul-de-sac lined with about thirty two-story houses dating from 1912. As unreal as it seemed to me, and it really did, I lived in one of those houses now. A long story that could be shortened into two words: Jean-Marc.

Almost everyone on Villa Daviel was in bed when I arrived. The subtle glow of televisions and bedside lamps crept through a few windows. I walked to number 22, opened the gate, climbed the staircase and slotted my key into the door. Inside my bag, my cell alerted me to a message, but I decided to stick to my getting home ritual, hang my scarf and jacket on the coat hook, leave my Doc Martens in their place—which meant next to the environmentally friendly sneakers belonging to the French architect, the ballet pumps belonging to the poet from Rio de Janeiro and Jean-Marc's worn ankle boots—and then finally go upstairs to my room.

Judging by the darkness under each door, everyone was asleep. I sat on the edge of my bed with my cell phone in my hand, immediately realizing that I'd be much more comfortable lying down, which I did, falling like a dead weight as I opened the message I had just received. It was from my dad. "Check it out, your brother's being mischievous." My dad loved using expressions like "check it out," "you get me" and "that's sick!" when speaking to people younger than himself, with all the naturalness of someone who had formulated the phrase half a dozen times in their head before releasing it dangerously in the middle of an unknown territory. I didn't have the heart to tell him that young people nowadays were no longer saying "sick," and that when he said "you get me" it sounded more like a poor attempt at a subtitle for a teenage movie.

There was a video attached. I opened it.

João Pedro was sitting on one of those little chairs for babies that have a large surface for gooey food. He was enthusiastically biting on a plastic rabbit, whose stomach issued a high-pitched squeak when it was pressed. João Pedro wasn't looking at the camera. In the background, I could hear a man (my dad) saying repeatedly: "Show us your tooth, son. Show us your tooth." He didn't show any teeth. One minute ten seconds of those rudiments of humanity. He was affectionate and clumsy, so I ended up laughing to myself and playing it again. However, as soon as the video restarted, it became clear that I was paying more attention to my dad's insistent voice than my brother's voracious oral phase. The natural tone, condescending, sweet, was enough to tell me that he wasn't bothered by the fact that he wasn't being acknowledged or even understood by his son. Anyway, I wondered whether it wasn't strange to start it all over again, to have a baby in the house and all the rest, after an interval of time that seemed long enough to have completely fallen out of practice.

I replied with something like "so cute," and got ready for bed.

The following morning, there was the suggestion of a sunny day outside. It had knocked on the window and now came in discreetly, scattering a kind of luminous powder over the objects arranged on the table: a pile of domestic gaucho paraphernalia that was rather disbelieving of its destiny. Next to the traditional black hat were the final versions of my sketches. I had never felt so satisfied with a piece of work than at that moment. For the umpteenth time, I looked at Jean-Marc. If he were a bit younger, I would send him knocking on the doors of some modeling agencies right away. Something he did with his eyes and eyebrows gave him an unpretentious and relaxed air, so that you might say that Jean-Marc felt more at ease now that when he was wearing his own clothes. Hands in pockets helped a bit too. I moved closer and adjusted Jean-Marc's *bombachas*, tucking them into his boots. The leather was cracking unevenly. The large peeling area on the right boot looked like a rodent in attack position.

"What do you think?" Jean-Marc asked, trying to locate himself in a distant mirror.

"Almost perfect."

He gave a short whistle.

"Looks perfect to me, Cora. Are you telling me you *made* this shirt?"

"Uh-huh."

Then he walked towards the mirror, stopped and began to laugh, his hair loose and rebellious as if he'd recently had a run in with the cold *minuano* wind.

"This is fabric from your land."

A raw cotton shirt, nice and tight. I had created the cuffs, the collar and the pocket from two neckerchiefs I bought in Bagé. The fabric was shiny like silk, with a delicate pattern and an elegant harmony of colors, which made it very difficult to imagine a gaucho using an accessory of that kind tied around his neck. It must have been a very special gaucho occasion to justify that almost feminine vanity. Anyway, now, integrated in the shirt, the neckerchiefs had definitely gone far beyond the borders of the pampa. The theatrical lead singer of an indie group would kill in that outfit. An artist who hung bicycle parts from museum ceilings would kill in that outfit. A writer whose whole book was a single sentence, five hundred pages long, with no commas would cause a lot of envy among his peers if he wore that outfit.

I was feeling tremendously proud of myself. And there were even more ambitious ideas in my sketches, which fortunately I wasn't required to execute. For example, the rustic hat with a band of spikes, the vest that alternated a smooth flannel with several embroidered pampa bands, tweed *bombachas*, capes.

Jean-Marc was looking at me.

"That's it!" I said. "I know what's missing, I've just realized. A bit of eyeliner and you'll be perfect."

"You're kidding."

"Just a little bit. No one will even notice."

"Why bother then?"

"Okay, they will notice. But only in a very positive way."

I said that as I rummaged through the drawers of a plastic organizer. Surprisingly enough, Jean-Marc stopped his retorts. He was actually giving me a bit of credit. In the third drawer, I found the charcoal pencil I was looking for. This pencil was a stub now, although I didn't remember having used it that much in my life; I think the last time had been at the birthday party for the Brazilian poet, and the penultimate time had certainly been much longer ago, months, one day on our trip to the interior, in the hotel room in São Francisco de Paula, where I had opened the wine bottle with my boot, it might have been there, but maybe I didn't actually care about the eyeliner, because then I saw a straight road with a rest stop in the background, it didn't last long at all, it gave way to the canyons, the gently rolling hills, the rail tracks, the abandoned house, and all before I could touch the water line of Jean-Marc's left eye.

"Careful with that."

Julia was arriving the following day. It was her first time in Paris and our first encounter in five months. I was trying not to worry about it. She had left her job at the *Montreal Gazette* and, on two separate occasions, had spoken to me about returning to Brazil, but it sounded like the typical speech ex-pats use when they idealize their native land too much, and in order to keep idealizing it they need to renounce it once and for all. The idea that Brazil was the country of the future only convinced those who weren't there.

"It's kind of intimate, putting eye make-up on someone, isn't it?"

"Quit moving."

Anyway, for the first time since I met her, Julia was showing signs of not knowing what to do next. And I must admit that that left me excited and full of hope. Perhaps she would stay. Perhaps I'd leave with her.

"Ready."

"Really ready? Can I blink again? I never thought I'd miss being able to do that."

"Look at me."

He obeyed.

"You're hot."

Jean-Marc examined his reflection in the mirror like a child struggling to recognize himself.

"If the girls like it."

"You need to promise me you won't fall in love with Julia."

"Does she speak French?"

"With a Quebecoise accent."

"Ah, of course. I'll try to understand."

"Jean-Marc, I'm serious."

"Hey, you don't need to tell me twice. Apart from anything else, why would she flirt with me when you're here? Look at yourself. My God, Cora."

Then I was embarrassed.

"Isn't it worth trying to be less insecure?"

"Not if the situation *begs* for insecurity. I'm talking about the girl who never told a soul that we had, I don't know, any kind of involvement. And you might find me very attractive or whatever—and stop pulling that face—but have you thought that that might not make the slightest bit of difference to her?"

"Can I laugh now?"

"What?"

"Can I laugh at what you've just said?"

I threw myself onto the bed. He pulled up a chair next to me.

"Cora, five months ago we sat in the gardens at Bastille with two bottle of rosé because you were sad *for no reason* (he was using my words), you were impossible the whole night, complaining about your course, your shitty job, your dad's wife. You complained about a guy playing the guitar because playing guitar in public was, according to your definition, the greatest affront to other people's liberty."

I remembered that night. Or, in truth, pieces of it. The guy with the guitar had looked very similar to a neighbor from my childhood, the oldest son of a couple of engineers, he had long hair when all the interesting boys had long hair, or at least the boys that I was interested in, that Company backpack slung over one shoulder, garage ramp skateboarder, tireless repeater of the intro to "Come As You Are," always up late and frequently flitting across the only illuminated window in his house. For a moment, I had thought it might even be him. We were all over Europe, living off those jobs we'd never accept if we weren't far away from home. Then I realized that he looked like my neighbor from eight, ten years earlier, not what he might potentially have become. My neighbor was now something very different to that nostalgic, out-of-context hologram.

"Listen . . ."

I think I had missed one or two sentences.

"Let me finish. I've always liked hanging out with you, Cora. Even on the days when you hate everything, you hate everything with a really passionate intensity, you know? At some point, I started telling you about Sophie. I had never told you before because you never asked directly, I said that maybe she was my lost love . . ."

"And I replied that you had lied to me about getting your tattoo retouched out of a 'deep respect' for your past."

Jean-Marc laughed.

"Julia came up right after that."

"What do you mean?"

"Doesn't matter. Well, you were a bit drunk at the time and you revealed all the spiciest details of your trip. I could barely cope with the richness of your descriptions."

"I know. That tends to happen with men."

"Basically, what I'm trying to say is that calling this girl hetero doesn't really cut it with me."

"When did I do that? Did I use the word hetero?"

"Not that word. But you said she probably wasn't attracted to you. Yes, in another way, that's what you meant."

"And what would you call her, Jean-Marc?"

He got up from the chair and drew back the curtains.

"At best, someone who doesn't have your courage."

There was a broad flight of stairs between two parallel streets, which smelled of urine. I sat on it. Sometimes someone would come down it, rarely alone, and from the type of person it was clear where they were going. The large glasses and beards could only mean Pop In. I was waiting for Julia on the fifth step from the top, next to the central handrail. There was some art on the walls on both sides, words on paper telling us to love one another, then a perfect pinball machine, then a girl lying on a cloud scattering who knows what kind of multicolored drops with her watering can. I was sure Julia was feeling a bit jet-lagged. But she wanted to see the city and see the night and see people asking strangers for cigarettes and the metro expelling more and more bodies.

Jean-Marc and Julia had met. That afternoon, he had taken it upon himself to lug her suitcase upstairs while the two of us lingered behind, Julia saying in Portuguese how she was dazzled by my little cul-de-sac, I mean, what are the chances of renting an actual house in Paris? I replied, almost embarrassed by my luck, that it was really a very remote chance. When we got upstairs, Jean-Marc was dragging the case to the foot of my bed. He hadn't bothered to use those little wheels, even on those perfectly smooth final yards. He looked at Julia and me, then rubbed his hands together, as if ready to receive instructions for another arduous task. There was no other task.

Jean-Marc was going to take a turn round the Saint-Ouen flea market because the afternoon looked as though it would turn nicer rather than worse, on a Parisian scale, of course, but

Julia and I had basic tourist spots to cover. She wanted to see the Eiffel Tower or the Seine or the Louvre or the Champs-Elysées to be absolutely sure where she was, which was something I could understand, as long as she didn't start posting photos of herself in front of those monuments as soon as she got there. I went to the bedroom door to say goodbye to Jean-Marc and he gave me one of those adolescent expressions of approval. That's the moment that you regret having shared confidences with a friend.

The afternoon was slightly strange and yet predictable. Not that it felt like a faithful copy of the first day of our trip to the interior, nor did it have any similarities in terms of, let's say, spontaneity as our starting point. A fresh start, I thought. A fresh start. I was allowing things to happen in their own time. So crossing a bridge over the Seine was still just a rehearsal for what might happen later. Julia seemed frightened. But I could stop acting selfishly and admit that not all her psychological states were necessarily related to me. After all, she had no job, she hadn't spoken to her brother since the fight, and all her best friends in Montreal tended to be Eric's friends. The best thing I could, and should do was to look like the best alternative.

Julia appeared holding a crepe as I remained sitting on the stairs between the two streets. Banana and Nutella. I had recommended it. She offered me a piece and I bit through the layers of soft dough, recognizing the lunches and dinners of my first months away from home. I handed the crepe back to her. Julia pointed at the corner of my mouth, without touching it, and told me I had Nutella on it. I had to clean it off myself. The sugar seemed to activate something in her after that, so we stayed on those stairs for longer than we needed to, the crepe gone, not complaining about the cold or the stench of urine, chatting like two people who meet to reminisce about the same things year after year. For a moment, Julia seemed to have forgotten that this was Paris, and that she had a whole load of cool things to do and a load of incredible places to see, golden angels blowing trumpets and the phallic legacy of an international fair. Could I have been jealous of my own city? Twenty or thirty minutes passed. Then I said it was time for us to go down the stairs. We took those few steps into my favorite bar, Pop In.

Initially, we squeezed into the room at the front. I was worried about bumping into Alejandra, which was slightly without foundation, because Alejandra had vanished from the map since our final conversation. Even though I was now an expert in that kind of conversation, I simply hated having to have them, and even more, I hated facing the possibility of encountering my exes again. She had cried! Alejandra had cried, who knows why. After the first tear, she reverted to speaking Spanish, her voice drawling on at length, with the clear intention of stretching out the conversation forever, or until one of us got up and left the café because she was exhausted and couldn't take any more, which is unfortunately what eventually happened.

As usual, most of Pop In's clientele was shouting in English. They would lean close in to the other person's ear to speak, so as to overcome the noisy fug of good music. They were tourists or foreigners who lived in Paris. The French didn't seem to like rock. They must have grown up thinking about something else, don't ask me what. The guys at the bar worked like two hyperactive marionettes, opening the beer taps and letting the golden liquid flow into pitchers that wouldn't look out of place in your grandmother's house, with ice tea, lemon and ice.

"What do you think?" I asked Julia, after having bought our drinks and returned with my physical and psychological integrity intact.

"About what?"

"This place."

She looked around her. A very tall man stuck a drinks stirrer shaped like a palm tree into a girl's cleavage.

"It could be a bar in Montreal."

"Everywhere looks the same."

"Minas do Camaquã?"

I smiled.

"Perhaps not there."

When we tried to follow the tall guy's advances again, it was already too late; the stirrer had returned to the drink, and the girl was holding her glass the way someone would hold a stranger's dirty sock. They weren't even talking to each other.

"Let's go upstairs," I said.

Five minutes later, three girls with bangs thought it was time to stretch their naked legs and dance to the next Swedish song destined never to become a hit, vacating a sofa in the process. We leaped onto it.

"Do you remember Sister Dulce?" Julia asked suddenly.

Which of the nuns was Sister Dulce? Perhaps the short one who sat at the entrance to the residence wearing civilian clothing. Or the one with the particularly small mouth like those women in the 20s who used lipstick to draw lips that were much smaller than their own, the difference being that this was a real nun's mouth, no tricks, no vanities, just the imperfect mouth God gave her. That wasn't Sister Dulce. That one was called Carmen, Clara, Celina or something like that. Sister Dulce was the nun who wore a light-gray habit and a ton weight of a cross; it would be easy to kneel with a piece like that, you'd probably just let yourself go, the hard thing would be staying upright. She wanted to catechize me, or at least I think that's what she was trying to do when sometimes she came up and started to quote Bible passages at me. I couldn't care less about Isaiah. Anyway, guess what? Julia had met Sister Dulce at the beach. Not just in the tiny center of the coastal town where her parents lived now, but on the actual beach, on the sand, dressed in her habit, wearing sandals, looking towards the horizon. The bottom of her robe was darker. She stood with her feet in the water. What was Sister Dulce doing there? Julia stood watching from a distance for quite a while, and yet the nun didn't move, and the wind was playing with her veil, and her skirt blew into an aerodynamic peak, and the waves were licking at her shins, but Sister Dulce stayed completely still looking out to sea. Perhaps because the ocean was such an incredible thing, making us think about Africa being right on the other side, even now no one has swallowed that con about the earth being round, I have to tell you something, I said all this to Julia and some more. Her immediate response was to give me a reserved smile. It wasn't by any means the end of her story. The following day, Julia was walking along the main street. Her dad had asked her to buy a bit of chicken heart for the barbecue, it was the only thing they still needed, and there was Julia, just about to enter the butcher's, when she realized that Sister Dulce was coming in the opposite direction. This time, like it or not, their eyes met. Of course Sister Dulce recognized Julia, how could she not when we gave the nuns so much trouble during those years, Julia wanted me to go up to her room with her but the rules of the residence stated that strangers were forbidden to enter the bedrooms, I wasn't a stranger, I was there all the time, I was a girl, after all, we just had to tidy up after ourselves, win over Sister Rose, if they wanted to baptize me, okay, let them baptize me then.

Sister Dulce had therefore recognized Julia. You don't go exchanging kisses on the cheek when you meet a nun, of course not, nor do you grab her hand, so the two of them maintained a certain distance, right by the door of the butcher's. How are you? Nice day, and so on, and then they moved on to what a coincidence: bumping into each other after so many years on that Santa Catarina beach. "My mother is ill," said the nun. Julia tried to calculate in her head how old Sister Dulce was, so as to have a vague idea of how old her mother must be, not all that old, she imagined, although it was always difficult to guess the age of someone who has taken a vow of chastity and only wears one outfit. "My mother is dying. She lives there," and she pointed to a three-story building like all the others. Julia swallowed drily. Why did Sister Dulce have to say that and in such a way? Apart from anything else, to be dying was a thousand times worse than having died. And Sister Dulce, Julia got the impression, didn't seem to be exactly resigned to it. Then Julia decided to say, less because she wanted to and more because nothing else came to her: "I saw you on the beach yesterday, looking at the sea." The nun smiled. She watched some people passing by, then turned back to Julia. "Yes, I went out to think for a bit. I was thinking." So she had been thinking! That whole time, standing on the beach, she had been thinking, not talking to God, having an incredible enlightening vision or anything like it.

"Is that the end of your story?" I asked.

"That's the end of my story, yes."

I looked at her. The chain with the Virgin Mary or saint-whatnot was still there, hanging round her neck.

"Kinda sad."

"You don't need to tell me, I know."

The second floor was much fuller now. People were almost tripping over our legs.

"But then, on the other hand, it's not like she's a friend of yours. I mean, it's sad, yeah, but it'll pass. Did she say anything like 'pray for my mother' or anything?"

"No."

I made myself comfortable on the sofa.

"Let me tell you. You might even see this as an unfortunate coincidence. I got a tattoo."

Julia raised her eyebrows as if that was the last thing she expected of me, which made no sense. I was talking about tattoos, not crepe dresses. I took off my jacket. I was wearing a sleeveless blouse underneath. The greenish sea wrapped around my right arm, with its pointy, synchronized little undulations. At the top, a large wave was forming.

"Oh my God, Cora, it's beautiful. It's perfect!"

She touched my arm with her fingertips.

"Fantastic grading. When did you do it?"

"About four months ago."

Julia smiled.

"Why the sea?"

"I don't know. I saw this illustration and thought it was nice. It's no more complex than that."

She thought about it for a bit.

"It's so great that you don't have some super explanation for your tattoo."

"What's the point in having an explanation? Time passes and the story you created in your head seems ridiculous."

"Are we still talking about tattoos?"

"Of course. Aren't we?"

I picked up my jacket and was about to put it on, but Julia blocked the maneuver with her hand saying: "leave it off." She kissed me. It was very quick and could have meant anything. Then, already on her feet, she said we should go to the dance floor. Was there a dance floor? Yes, there was. We crossed the entire second floor until we reached the narrow staircase. It was a really tight squeeze, no bigger than a garage, and dark, and sweltering. I was a bit giddy, trying to synchronize my legs to the bubblegum song. A few guys were watching us and I kept averting my eyes, I span around, I averted my eyes, span a bit more, averted my eyes again. Now and then I came face-to-face with Julia. She seemed to be really enjoying herself, she bopped her head and her bangs shook, her hips understood the music perfectly, two or three times she raised her arms, I mean she was really enjoying herself like crazy, but at the same time it was as though she wasn't there, not entirely, so I decided not to be there either. Home. At that time, my concept of home had been diluted, my old house was now, out of convention, referred to as my mother's house, that was the house I was thinking about, and everything began in the dark. In the early hours on our street, there were howls from dogs and sometimes we heard crickets. Anything more than that sent us into a start of alert. I went downstairs foot in front of foot, entered the kitchen, felt my way along the counter until I reached the refrigerator. When I found the bottle of water, the whole ensemble of fluorescent lights came on.

"Hi," said my mom. She was standing at the door in a nightdress.

"I thought you were asleep."

"I woke up when you got in. You plural. Is there a girl in your room, Cora?"

"She's not feeling too well."

"You shouldn't drink so much. And drive."

"I'm fine, mom."

She took an apple from the fruit bowl by the stalk, looked at it, apparently for no reason, then put it back in the bowl.

"Who's the girl?"

"She's a classmate from college. She's from the interior. She lives here in a residence, like with nuns."

I laughed, but she didn't.

"Switch off the light when you go to bed, yeah?"

I stayed there a while longer, also for no reason, then I returned to my bedroom. The TV was still on mute, it was a western, full of flies and stubbly chins, but Julia had only seen the first fifteen minutes. She said that she loved cowboys. Now she was stretched out on my bed and it didn't look like there was much room left for me. I took off my clothes, put on an old t-shirt and tried to get comfortable as best I could. The film was still a long way from finishing. I kept watching. A duel. A romance. A desert. That girl sleeping at my side. We all loved cowboys.

CAROL BENSIMON was born in the southern Brazilian city of Porto Alegre in 1982. She is the author of a story collection and three novels. In 2012 she was selected by *Granta* as one of the Best Young Brazilian Novelists. This is her first book to appear in English.

BETH FOWLER has been a freelance translator since 2009, working from Portuguese and Spanish to English, and has a degree in Hispanic Studies from the University of Glasgow. Her published translations include *Open Door* and *Paradises* by Iosi Havilio, and *Ten Women* by Marcela Serrano. She lives near Glasgow, Scotland, with her husband and two children.

Transit Books is a nonprofit publisher of international and American literature, based in Oakland, California. Founded in 2015, Transit Books is committed to the discovery and promotion of enduring works that carry readers across borders and communities. Visit us online to learn more about our forthcoming titles, events, and opportunities to support our mission.

TRANSITBOOKS.ORG